Praise for *We Were Witches*

"Forget Freytag's Pyramid (of Predictable Male Prose) —behold Gore's Upside-Down Triangle (of Fierce Feminist Narrative)! Drawing from myth, fairy tale, the wisdom of third wave literary icons, and the singular experiences of a queer single mama artist trying to survive the nineties, *We Were Witches* is its own genre, in its own canon. It moves with punk rock grace and confidence, and I totally loved it."

KATE SCHATZ

"Gore's portrait of the artist as a young witch seizes the shame and hurt internalized by young women and turns it into magic art and poetry. Ariel Gore's writing is a diamond pentacle carved into a living heart, transforming singular experience into universal knowledge."

SUSIE BRIGHT

"Ariel Gore's *We Were Witches* beguiles the very shape of classical narrative by jamming into it the unapologetic and glorious story of a queer single mother's body. The fact of this body and the stories generated from it exposes just how it is that the narrative models we inherit literally incarcerate and murder some souls while in favor of the ascension and sanctity of others— specifically, white heterosexual heroes and their plot

fitting actions. I say burn the whole house down. *We Were Witches* reminds us to resist. One woman's body refusing to become property, refusing to be overwritten by law or traditions; one woman's body cutting open a hole in culture so that actual bodies might emerge. A triumphant body story. A singularly spectacular siren song."

LIDIA YUKNAVITCH

"Ariel Gore's *We Were Witches* is both magical and punk rock—the way it takes traditional values and traditional story structure to task, the way Gore's protagonist, Ariel, uses witchy intelligence to resist a system totally against her."

MICHELLE CRUZ GONZALES

"*We Were Witches* is raw and truthful, painfully funny, inspiring of outrage, and alive with the wonder and magic of a feminist awakening. One single mom becoming woke, struggling, and triumphing on her own outsider terms, *We Were Witches* is a new feminist classic, penned by one of the culture's strongest authors at her most experimental and personal."

MICHELLE TEA

We Were Witches

ALSO BY ARIEL GORE

The End of Eve

All the Pretty People

Bluebird: Women and the New Psychology of Happiness

How to Become a Famous Writer Before You're Dead

The Traveling Death and Resurrection Show

Whatever, Mom

Atlas of the Human Heart

The Mother Trip

The Hip Mama Survival Guide

We Were Witches

A NOVEL BY ARIEL GORE

FEMINIST
PRESS
AT THE CITY UNIVERSITY
OF NEW YORK
NEW YORK CITY

Published in 2017 by the Feminist Press
at the City University of New York
The Graduate Center
365 Fifth Avenue, Suite 5406
New York, NY 10016

feministpress.org

First Feminist Press edition 2017

 This book was made possible thanks to a grant
from New York State Council on the Arts with
the support of Governor Andrew Cuomo and the
New York State Legislature.

First printing September 2017

Cover and text design by Drew Stevens
Cover and interior illustrations by Suki Boynton

Library of Congress Cataloging-in-Publication Data

Names: Gore, Ariel, 1970- author.
Title: We were witches / by Ariel Gore.
Description: First Feminist Press edition. | New York, NY : Feminist Press,
    2017.
Identifiers: LCCN 2017006474 (print) | LCCN 2017010982 (ebook) | ISBN
    9781558614338 (paperback) | ISBN 9781936932023 (ebook)
Subjects: | BISAC: FICTION / Contemporary Women. | FICTION / Com-
ing of Age. |
    FICTION / Lesbian.
Classification: LCC PS3607.O5959 W4 2017 (print) | LCC PS3607.O5959
(ebook) |
    DDC 813/.6--dc23

*Some folks climb a mountain
to get where they're going,
and the rest of us, well,
we're clawing to get the fuck out
of a hole we didn't dig.*

—LIZ HENRY

BOOK 1

Invocations

Gore Girl

When I was born, my mother was so horrified to be handed a female baby that she took three months to name me. My birth certificate just says "Gore Girl."

I have the copy of Sylvia Plath's *Ariel* my mother read when she was pregnant with me.

She highlighted just one stanza in just one poem: *I am terrified by this dark thing / That sleeps in me; / All day I feel its soft, feathery turnings, its malignity.*

When *Ariel* was published, Sylvia Plath had already killed herself—a casualty of the soft, feathery war between art and motherhood. In the book's title poem, a child's cry "melts in the wall" as the poet flies on by, an arrow on her horse, a hope, free and suicidal.

As I grew up, my mother would tell me she named me Ariel so I could pass for a man on paper. She said Ariel was a man's name.

But I have the book.

I know that I'm not just a failed man.

I am at once the malignity and the escape.

Other Starting Points

Things the world has taught me to feel ashamed of:

1. Being born a female body.
2. My sexuality—the whole of it.
3. Motherhood.
4. Scars and stretch marks.
5. Debt: $127,862 in outstanding student loans, still snowballing at 8.25 percent interest from a $32K original loan.
6. My art (mostly stories).

Things I have in fact felt ashamed of:

1. All items listed above.
2. Artistic failure.
3. Also, success when it draws too much attention.

Freytag's Pyramid

My creative writing instructor stood up fast, nearly tripping over the ragged hem of her full-length purple skirt. She grabbed a piece of white chalk, drew a giant penis on the blackboard, tapped her heels on the floor, and said, "This is a pyramid." Her lipstick edged slightly over the boundaries of her lips, and I wondered if she'd tried to make them seem fuller with the edging or if she just didn't see very well.

I glanced at the other women in the workshop.

Was the illustration on the blackboard not obviously a penis?

I'd been allowed into the graduate workshop as an undergrad. Maybe best not to ask too many questions.

The instructor dragged the white chalk up one side of the penis. "You begin with the rising action," she explained. She drew a quick circle around the head of the penis. "It culminates in *climax!*"

The other women in the class nodded like they'd heard it all before, like they totally didn't see the penis.

I jotted a note, pushed it toward the poet sitting next to me: *I'm gonna put a vagina in the middle of my story, not the head of a penis.*

The poet glanced at my note, but didn't seem to read it.

*

La Figa
Ariel Gore
Creative Writing Workshop 201

In the front passenger's seat of Rosella's little silver
hatchback, I clutched the paperback copies of *Spiritual
Midwifery* and *Natural Childbirth* that had arrived in
the lavender-scented care package from California. My
fear takes the shape of every cypress silhouette in the
Tuscan night. *Where are we going?* Dark roads curve
through stone mountains. The books said the pain
would come in waves. This pain is not waves.

The books said I could trust my body.

Where? To a hospital where they speak a language
not my own and I won't remember the word for "push."

Had I ever known the word?

No natural light. No soothing music.

I repeat aloud the only words I can remember in the
foreign language: *"No farmaci, no droga."*

The clock on the hospital wall is large and it bends
and morphs like Dali's clock, exploding on the ledge of
my girlhood.

I lay on my back, open my legs.

The nurse's gloved hand reaches inside me. *"Che
tempo,"* she says, her voice soft, her words hard, her
face blurred.

The books said try and sleep, but who can sleep with
this pressure erupting between spine and belly? The
books said I would reconnect with the goddess Artemis

tonight, but crucifixes hang on the hospital walls and my boyfriend smells like whiskey.

"Go away," I mumble.

"Fine, if you don't want me here." And a door slams shut.

Now cold shower and sudden clamor, now yelling in the language I can't remember. A wheelchair. The clock on the ledge. Morning light blinds. A man is angry. Nurses scurry to move my body like moving my body will make the man unangry. Fluorescent lights blind. A cold metal table at my naked back. Metal stirrups tighten. And still this pressure. "*No farmaci, no droga.*" I chant the words like a mantra.

Nurses scream shrill, "*Spingere!*"

A wide leather strap at my belly. They're tying me down tighter. Tighter still. What does the word mean? *Spingere.*

It's a word written on doors.

Surely some part of me knows this word.

Surely no part of me wants to push my newborn into the hands of an angry man.

I'm naked and tied down. The nurses have my arms now. The nurses have my shoulders. My legs shake and the nurses hold my legs as they yell more words I don't understand. Stone hospital, and the crucifix swells against the wall and a woman calls from the hallway, "*Benedetta?*"

She stumbles into the doorway of my bright delivery room, her nightgown covered in blood, and she's crying, "*Mia figlia sia morta.*" She falls onto her knees and someone—another woman—pulls her away.

"*Benedetta?*"

I am bright dark pain pull dream bent clock.

Now the angry man stands between my legs, his eyes glowing yellow gray.

I blink into his face and into the sound of the women screaming.

My own scream becomes a moan, then goes silent as the man shoves the pointed blade of his steel surgical knife into my unmedicated teenage cunt and cuts a hard left.

As the blade slices through the wall of my vagina, it sears hot like molten iron, then cold as everything goes dark.

A starched nurse holds my baby.

My baby blinks wide-eyed surprised silence desire.

I pull against the metal and leather restraints to reach for her.

And in that blinding false light of morning, the doctor hits her. The sound of his open palm against her skin is a sound I will not forget. The doctor wants to hear my baby cry. The only alive the doctor knows is crying.

My baby cries. She is alive.

The woman in the bloody nightgown calls from the doorway, "*In vita!*"

Alive means they hit you.

I reach for *mia figlia in vita* because I have to tell her that alive means your mother will hold you, too, but they splash her with cold water away from me and she cries, alive.

The other woman cries, too. Benedetta is not alive.

By midday, the clock will appear round on the wall again and my baby will sleep in a bassinet next to my narrow hospital bed and the nurses will all mock me: "*No farmaci, no droga!*" And they'll laugh and shake their heads and glance at my daughter and call her "*poverina*" and "*zingara.*"

The other mother steps into my doorway, her bloody nightgown clean now. A nurse holds her by both shoulders as she reaches toward my baby's bassinet and speaks in a language I understand clearly: she knows my baby is not hers, but she wants to hold her.

I curl my hand to invite Benedetta's mother into my room.

The nurses watch, nervous, but Benedetta's mother just places one hand on my baby's small chest and whispers, "*In vita.*"

Later, the doctor will appear to ask my boyfriend, sober now, if he thinks they should sew up my vagina. The doctor offers to make it tighter than before.

And my boyfriend points to my crotch and says, "*Si, si, la figa.* Sew it up."

So a nurse I've never seen before sits between my legs and stitches me, laughing to herself—"*no farmaci, no droga*"—as she embroiders my unmedicated inner labia with her thick needle.

I stare vacantly at the doctor and my boyfriend as pain blooms through my body like nausea.

"Cut *them*," I whisper to no one. And maybe I close my eyes for a moment because just then I hear a faraway clamor of hooves on cobblestones. As the sound gets closer, the church bells outside begin to clang. I look up to the hospital-room window just as the glass shatters and Artemis appears—head of a goddess, body of a deer—a day late, shooting arrows into necks of the doctor and my boyfriend. They both fall, bleeding from their jugulars.

The nurse looks up, startled, and freezes midstitch.

I gesture toward the fallen men as Artemis rides on. "Sew *them* up," I say to the nurse with her needle, and I close my legs.

*

Later still—seventeen and a half years later—I'll have my legs spread for a midwife in Portland, Oregon, because I'm knocked up again, this time with the help of borrowed sperm in a yogurt cup, and the midwife will squint in the soft natural light and she'll say, "Oh. My. Goodness. Is that a mediolateral episiotomy?"

And my breath will catch in my throat and I'll whisper weakly, "Yes," and I'll be surprised that an ancient scar I didn't ask for still holds so much shame.

The midwife in Oregon will gasp a quick inhale and she'll reach for me fast as if to touch my scar, but she'll stop short and instead ask, "Where on earth did you get that?"

And I'll say, "Rural Italy, 1990."

"Would. You. Mind?" the midwife will breathe, cautious, like she's discovered a rare archeological site. "If. I. Bring. In. A. Few. Students? To. See. This?"

And I'll swallow hard against the tears as four women in white coats gather between my legs and their teacher points and lectures, "This is the routine genital mutilation you've read about in early to mid-twentieth-century Western obstetrics. They cut to the side rather than downward through the perineum—so the patient likely experienced excruciating pain and often tremendous blood loss. As you can see, it wasn't even stitched with dissolvable sutures.

"This.

May.

Actually.

Be.

Silk."

I'll glance up at the wall as the clock begins to bend.

The women in white coats will stare between my legs, and they'll *aah*, and they'll *hmm*, and I'll know they all want to touch it. But not one of them will have the nerve.

My body is a curio shop.

*

That creative writing instructor, with her ragged purple skirt and her lipstick edging over the boundaries of her lips, didn't like my birth story with the vagina right in the middle of it. She said, "Ariel, I'm not seeing the pyramid."

*

It was just a few years after I took that class that I started publishing essays and stories and zines and books, and started going out and doing readings and planning zine tours and book tours, and started traveling with bands and other writers or with puppeteers, and always traveling with my daughter, Maia, too, of course.

And here was America, neon lit and dusty.

And here were my social anxieties.

When I started publishing, sometimes the projects brought with them fat checks and sometimes the projects brought with them slim checks and sometimes the projects brought with them no checks at all. Or like, you know, *The check is in the mail.*

And here was America, capitalist and anti-artist.

And here were my rent and utility bills.

When I started publishing, I thought my career would trace rising action like that creative writing instructor's chalk-drawn plot structure that looked like a penis—and culminating in an impressive climax—

But
maybe
you can't
expect your
career to form the
shape of a penis if you
don't actually have one.

*

Take me back to that graduate writing workshop, but this time with a voice. I have some questions for my instructor. I will raise my hand. I will speak when called on.

Professor, what is the true shape of experience?

What is the shape of successful failure, of vulnerability and humiliation, of inexplicable joy?

What is the shape of a story that maps the cultural tyranny of what it means to be a girl child and a woman mother and a woman intellect and a woman creator in a world built from male paradigms?

Professor, my arc isn't rising.

The first urge is to shape the story into a vagina—in opposition to the shape of a penis—because the first urge is *fuck you*, and that's how they taught us to fuck.

*

When I was a kid, there were naked women all over my house.

My mother and her best friend, Roberta, were going through their vulva phase.

I'd tumble in from elementary school and there'd be one naked woman splayed out across the live-edge oak coffee table, another sitting, back straight, in a wicker armchair, another frozen in some tai chi pose by the front window.

Roberta drew the naked women's portraits in charcoal.

My mother sculpted their bodies in wax, planned to cast them in bronze.

Sometimes the naked women were plump and sometimes the naked women were thin, but the naked women were always younger than my mom and Roberta, and always older than me.

"Hi, Tiniest," my mother said as I set down my green backpack.

"Hi, Ariel," Roberta called from her easel.

I smiled awkward, unsure if I'd walked in on something or what.

"We're about to sit down to tea and oysters," my mother offered.

"Oh, all right," I said.

At our round dining-room table, the naked women sat silent, now wearing light-colored robes.

I stared at a raw oyster in its shell on the plate in front of me.

"Ariel, just eat the whole vagina," my mother admonished me.

And so I did.

It tasted good.

Salty and citrus.

"I brought vulva biscuits," Roberta announced, all singsongy as she rose up from her place at the table and glided into the kitchen and back out again carrying a red plate of sugar cookies each shaped like the oysters. She pointed to the nuances of their form: "The outer labia, the inner labia, the clitoris . . . Ariel, try one!"

I reached for the plate. My fingernails were bitten down to their nubs. I brought the cookie to my mouth. It tasted like vanilla and maple, but I felt funny.

It was 1979 or 1980. Judy Chicago's epic vulva-plate installation, *The Dinner Party*, had just arrived at the San Francisco Museum of Modern Art.

Judy Chicago, were you their influence?

Judy Chicago, I think I had a really weird fourth-grade year because of you.

I mean, I liked your dinner party.

Believe me, I ate the whole vagina.

But what if this genital obsession doesn't have to be the only taste?

*

When I sent my Gammie Gore a postcard telling her I was pregnant at age eighteen, she wrote to my father on a brown card: *Ariel tells me she's pregnant. I think that's very irresponsible.*

When I called her a few months later to ask if she wanted to meet the baby, my Gammie Gore said, "Isn't it a shame?"

My Gammie Gore wore slacks and sensible sweaters and I loved her beyond reason, but now her unhappiness flooded my veins.

I swallowed hard and tasted copper.

My Gammie Gore and my Grandpa Gore had a wealth I'd never know. Both their fathers had been copper-mining engineers in Chile and in Anaconda, Montana, where "The Company," as they called it, extracted hundreds of millions of dollars' worth of metal from the earth just as Thomas Edison's light bulb sparked demand for endless miles of copper wire across the country. Both my Gammie Gore's and Grandpa Gore's families went up to Montana to profit from the destruction of the earth there—they weren't from the area, didn't happen upon it by chance. Their families met there in the shadows of the smokestacks, so my father is the direct result of the intentional human destruction of the earth for profit.

No destruction of the earth = no my father.

No my father = no me.

Isn't that right?

Cut into the earth, slap the baby, and see if she cries alive.

"The Company" was later responsible for the pump-and-dump stock market manipulation that helped to create the Great Depression of the 1930s.

But my Gammie Gore did not say *It's a shame* about those things.

She did not think those things were irresponsible.

The Anaconda stack, 585 feet of phallocratic reality, still dominated the landscape of my grandparents' town, but the soil and rivers and topless mountains and strip-mine pits were contaminated with arsenic and acid and copper sulfate *and god help the migrating snow geese that stop at the Berkeley Pit outside Butte,*

Montana, thinking that a round of bright blue is the international symbol for fresh water.

As a teenager, my Grandpa Gore had bone cancer, which may or may not have been the result of metal poisoning, so he had his leg amputated, which made him feel weird and ashamed about his body forever and always after that—but he survived it all to be a man like they told him to and to cofound a huge defense contractor that would make all the world's B-2 stealth bombers and Black Widow night fighters and cruise missiles. But my Gammie Gore did not say *It's a shame* about that.

She did not think that was irresponsible.

Instead, my Gammie Gore felt ashamed of my grandpa's body and the way it had been cut. My Gammie Gore felt ashamed of my father's schizophrenia, too, which may or may not have been the result of metal poisoning. And now my Gammie Gore felt ashamed of me and of my teenage motherhood.

I sat with that.

I needed to sit with that for a long time.

I sat with the baby on Carmel Beach, not far from my grandparents' little yellow house, and the two of us looked out to the ocean.

What would happen if we inverted Freytag's pyramid?

Maybe the opposite of a phallus isn't a vagina, but a strip mine.

What would happen if we abandoned both genitalia and strip mine when it came to envisioning the true shape of experience?

We might symbolize creativity as a brain,
a hand,
an eye,
a heart,
a cell,
a seed,
a spore,
an ocean,
a mother and child looking out to the ocean.

We might symbolize creativity as a body of water,
a body of work,
a body of resistance—toxic with all the ways we've turned ourselves.

We might build a book like this.

Salvage Your Skin

I was three months pregnant when I got to Rome. I'd dropped out of high school and been traveling and working—mostly broke—around Asia and Europe for three years and now I was knocked up.

My black eye had faded into a pretty mustard color.

At the post office, the woman behind the counter inspected my passport, then handed me two brown padded envelopes addressed in my mother's familiar looped handwriting.

The first envelope contained a paperback copy of *The Scarlet Letter* by Nathaniel Hawthorne, no note, like maybe I should name the baby Pearl.

The second envelope contained seven tubes of lotion and a note that read,

Tiniest,

John tells me you're pregnant and keeping the baby. I went straight to the Clarins counter at Macy's. The saleswoman told me that youthful teenage skin is THE MOST PRONE TO STRETCH MARKS because it isn't yet elastic.

I hope I am not too late, Tiniest. I am begging you. At least salvage your skin.

I've enclosed:
 Stretch Mark Minimizer
 Stretch Mark Control
 Body Lift Cellulite Control
 Body Contour Treatment Oil
 Bust Beauty Lotion
 Bust Beauty Firming Lotion
 Bust Beauty Extra-Lift Gel
 Slather it on, Tiniest. I'm begging you. At least salvage your skin!
 Love,
 Mom

Outside the post office, I lit a cigarette. I took a few drags, then crushed the burning cherry of it into the exposed skin of my chest.

I didn't yet have the language to say, *Take that, Freytag.*

Streetlights

There was just one rule for being ten: get home before the streetlights come on or you're gonna get slapped across the face in front of whoever has come to dinner.

But you're ten years old and you love that dusky walk home like a tomato. You love the darkening light, the temperature drop, the warm wind on your cheeks, the first stars beginning to bright.

Most nights you duck in through the back door with moments to spare before those pink-yellow streetlights come on. But nights like tonight—*Shit.*

You must have been dusk-dreaming.

You must have forgotten to pick up your pace.

You're a block from home when those damn streetlights come on.

Make a plan. Don't think twice. Slap your own face. Slap it hard. *Slap.* Make it sting. *Slap.* Make it strong. *Slap.* Because it's one thing to get slapped across the face in front of whoever's come to dinner but it's totally another thing to cry in front of them.

You will not cry in front of them.

If the grown-ups thought they could make you cry on demand, well, the grown-ups have another thing coming.

You're in fourth grade. You know long division. You know how to spell *science* and other words with silent letters. You know about oysters and vulva biscuits. And you know this: the grown-ups have another goddamn thing coming.

Creep in through the back door. Let it slam shut behind you. Slip off your white Keds. Creep—carpet to hardwoods.

The house smells like weed. Sweet and musty. Smells more like weed than usual.

The voices from the dining room laugh.

It's Pink Floyd on the stereo instead of Joan Baez.

Slap yourself again. Right palm to left cheek. And again. Left palm to right cheek.

You're ready.

Don't cry.

Be a man.

Step into the dining room, fully prepared. Clench your fists at your sides.

But this time the grown-ups just look up at you from their eggplant spinach Parmesan and their glasses of red wine and they smile.

Your mother says, "Hi, Tiniest."

You smile back your chipped-tooth smile. It's like none of the grown-ups even know the streetlights have come on. Like they weren't even paying the least bit of attention.

Someone who has come to dinner says, "Eggplant spinach Parmesan?"

And you say, "No, thank you. I already ate." And you turn away from the grown-ups so they won't see your eyes begin to tear up.

Later, you'll remember the way your face stung and you'll pinpoint this night as the night you became one of them, and you'll mourn your treason, because someday you'll grow up and you'll run away from them, and someday they'll grow old, and they'll cough blood and die, but the bully part of them that hated you will live on inside of you, and you'll know that you colluded with them against yourself, and you'll slap yourself again. Hard. But you won't cry. Because now it will be your own fault. Just like they always said.

Look what you made me do.

*

It's usually at night now, after the streetlights come on, but not always at night. The pillowy ashamed feeling descends from somewhere behind me, free-floating at first. When it alights on my back, right between my shoulder blades, the pressure feels hot like iron branding my skin. It pushes through with a *pop*. It blocks my throat, then flash floods into my bloodstream. It tastes like copper, but my mouth feels dry. The color of the feeling is red.

The voices come in whispers at first: *What have you done now, Ariel? Everyone is very embarrassed for you.*

It's your ill-planned pregnancy.

The money you owe.

Your arrest record.

Surely a diagnosis.

It's this essay.

And what happened last night after that bottle of wine.

It's the time you were raped, which you recently stopped calling "my rape" in hopes that disowning it linguistically might distance it to abandoned memory.

It's your waistline.

Your unrealistic rendition of a red-winged blackbird in black ink.

And all the rest of your terrible drawings.

It's that you offend people, Ariel.

You're too quiet.

People know your mother hits you.

They know your father's crazy.

They know your stepdad got excommunicated for marrying your mom.

Blood stains on white pants.

Your bingeing, your purging.

Your privilege, your poverty.

It's, "Don't cry. Be a man."

It's, "Smile. Like a lady."

It's your sexuality.

Obviously.

Credit card declined.

Your unzipped fly.

Your kid throwing a tantrum.

Toilet paper stuck to your shoe.

Did you seriously just write that in your book, Ariel?

It's the bad thing inside you, hot with desire that everyone can see.

As the voices get louder, I begin to recognize them. *Oh, hey*, I laugh nervous, oddly relieved by the familiarity. They're the voices of my parents and my grandparents and my aunts and my ancestors and the boyfriends and bullies of my girlhood. Most of the people the voices belong to are dead now, but I can still hear them.

I think it's because we're built from each other.

For better or for worse, we're all built from each other.

I pull a copy of *Leaves of Grass* down from my bookshelf because "Song of Myself" can usually ground me enough to quiet the voices. I read aloud: *For every atom belonging to me as good belongs to you.* And I close my eyes into my shame and my desire.

For every atom belonging to me as good belongs to you.

That's for sure.

Career Counseling

I don't like those people who tell kids that adolescence is the best years of our lives.

That's the kind of lie that can really kill you. It's the kind of lie that makes you feel alone in your depression. It's the kind of lie that can scare you for a long time.

There were other lies like that.

"I think I want to be a writer," I told the career counselor at the California junior college where I almost signed up for classes.

I sat across from her in her little gray office.

She wore a well-ironed gray suit.

A poster behind her pictured the Everest summit: AIM HIGH.

She stared at me, silent.

Aim high, I mouthed to myself, tasting the irony of it all. I didn't tell the counselor I'd crossed the Himalayas by myself on foot when I was seventeen. Before the baby. "You know, write?" I said. "Creative writing?"

The career counselor shook her head and her exhale held a silent, bitter laugh. She let the corners of her mouth turn up as she said, "Good *luck.*"

I just sat there, not saying anything. I glanced over at Maia asleep in her soft blue onesie in her blue polka-dot stroller.

The counselor leaned back in her gray chair and adjusted her gray jacket and tilted her gray head to the side like she was maybe trying to pop a vertebra in her neck and she said, "Miss Gore." She looked down at the piece of paper on her desk, like maybe she was trying to remember my first name; she said, "Ariel." She said, "Miss Gore, you have a child to take care of now. You really ought to make an attempt to come down to earth and think about that. You need to think about your child and you need to ask yourself how you're going to make a living."

There was a small stack of brochures on that gray desk that invited: *Become a Certified Electrician.*

I nodded a few times too many. I stood up slowly, hunched over like I was looking at the baby when really I just didn't want to look at the counselor.

Her words made my heart contract, but I still felt compelled to politeness. "Thank you," I said before I grabbed the handles of the polka-dot stroller. I opened the door to get out of that airless office, held it open with my hip as I maneuvered the stroller.

The career counselor didn't rise to help me.

"Thank you," I said again, and I let the door slam shut behind me.

Why did you say thank you, Ariel?
You're an idiot, Ariel.
Shut up, only crazy people talk to themselves, Ariel.

I pushed the stroller, my pace quickening. My mother's words rattled in my head too.

You chose this life, Ariel.

You're on your own, Ariel.

Everyone is very embarrassed for you.

Like I'm nineteen and I've already lost, no unlosing now.

The cement path led past cement pillars, past square gardens, toward a green expanse. "Aim high," I whispered under my breath, then tasted the rage. "That fucking bitch." My walk morphed into a run. Tears streamed down my face. I pushed the stroller. Maia slept. She kept on sleeping. I felt like a sucker for telling that counselor woman what I wanted, what I wanted to be. I felt like a fool for wanting something I had no right to want anymore.

Hadn't I once been a flat-chested kid, knobby skinned knees, and safe in my body? My skin streaked with blood and mud, I used to collect tadpoles in a mason jar at the rocky edge of the San Francisquito Creek. I kept my hair short. Only my mother knew I was a girl.

I felt very far from that child body now.

Maybe the career counselor was right. Maybe I didn't know how to live. I didn't know how to make a living.

It didn't matter if I could make stories.

I had to make a living.

But becoming an electrician scared me. Electrocution

scared me. I felt too anxious and afraid—I should have told that counselor—to be trusted with live wires.

I was back living with my mother and stepfather in the stucco house I'd run away from, trying to pretend I didn't notice the sour stench of my own humiliation.

I got a chain letter in the mail.

I sent ten dollars to the name at the top of the list.

I added my name to the bottom of the list and sent it off to ten unsuspecting members of my stepfather's church congregation.

Surely if I waited, I would receive $10,000 in ten dollar increments—small white envelopes in the mail.

College was a distant plan B. It was a someday thing. A not-now thing. I awaited my $10,000, but all that came in the mail was a Stonehenge postcard from the baby's father.

Dear Ariel,

In Londontown hanging with Joe Strummer. Almost have the money together for the airfare to San Francisco. Sorry about everything. Let's start new.

Love,
Lance

I threw the postcard away.

I'd always had a soft spot for the baby's father. He sang that David Bowie song, "Kooks," in the morning in his sweet London accent, but he was a mean drunk at night, and even though I didn't know about alcoholism yet, I could see that the drinking was getting worse. I could see something else too—something I couldn't quite put my finger on—something about the way the world kept telling him to "be a man" that frustrated him to the point of violence.

In the morning light through the kitchen window, my mother made fresh zucchini and peach baby food. She had painted my childhood bedroom pink. She held Maia in her manicured hands, said we could stay as long as we needed.

But at night she said the opposite. "Everyone," she whispered, "is very embarrassed for you, Ariel."

Who was everyone?

I imagined a whole audience of everyone I'd ever met, spotlight on me, and they all cringed knowing I'd done something terribly wrong.

I share my childhood bed
with the baby
nurse her as we both fall asleep
her body is soft like clay
all hunger

The next morning my mother breathed angry like it might as well be night. "Unwed mother," she seethed as if she were only talking to herself now. "This is not happening."

Was this?
Not happening?

My mother shook her head. "Oh, let's just have tea."

Her best friend, Roberta, appeared in the entryway, her long, sand-colored hair braided into a rope.

Yes, let's just have tea with Roberta.

I stood in the tiled kitchen, Maia on my hip. She could hold her own head up now, and she gripped the sleeve of my black T-shirt with her tiny hands.

Waiting for the water to boil, I arranged boxes of herbal tea. *Red Zinger, Grandma's Tummy Mint, Almond Sunset.*

"You have to get out of here," Roberta hissed at me under the whistle of the kettle.

My mother had just stepped out the French doors to pick a lemon.

"Out," Roberta hissed, louder.

"Why?" I said without looking up. *Peach Passion. Sleepy Time. Orange Spice.* "It's beautiful here," I said, "and elm shaded." I didn't tell Roberta I was waiting for my $10,000 in little white envelopes.

"Out." Roberta glared at me with round possum eyes. "Jealousy is dangerous. Your mother is dangerous." Roberta bared her teeth and for an odd moment I thought she might bite my shoulder.

I stepped back.

Roberta seemed to shrink, just a little.

"Roberta?"

Roberta was crazy, I knew that, but she was right. Pink paint couldn't quite cover the angry thing. Her face suddenly became more pointed, and short white hair sprouted on her cheeks and chin.

"Roberta?"

"In another time," she whispered, "if your family

had any money to speak of, you'd have been sent off to a home, your baby stolen from you, and no one ever would have spoken of it again." Her cheeks flushed a shade of dark red I hadn't seen before, then turned white as she now shrank very quickly.

I felt disoriented as Roberta kept shrinking. Hadn't I just been about to pour boiling water into tea mugs?

"Roberta?"

She was a possum on my mother's tiled kitchen floor, the size of a house cat but the shape of a rat.

"Roberta?"

The possum made a hissing sound as she breathed. She looked up at me and then scurried across the room and out through the laundry room. She scratched at the back door.

I felt panicky, pushed the door open for her.

She looked back up at me one more time before she ran across the dead grass and under the neighbor's fence.

The neighbor's dog barked.

I rushed to the fence, Maia still on my hip. I peered through the gap between two boards. And there was the possum who had been Roberta, flat on her back like she was dead, the neighbor's dog pawing her.

I kept watching.

The dog walked away.

The possum rolled over onto her belly, stood up on her short little legs, and scurried off.

"Where's Roberta?" my mother asked back inside her tiled kitchen.

I shrugged. "She said she had an appointment."

My mother nodded, a little confused, then bared her teeth at me so quickly I wasn't sure if I'd imagined it. She hissed.

Did my mother hiss?

I looked at my pyramid of boxed tea.

Possum, I thought. Possums play dead. Possums lie low. *Better aim low for a while, Ariel. Better play dead.*

That evening over spaghetti with fresh basil, Maia played with her noodles and I told my mother and step-father I'd been accepted to an alternative college up in the North Bay.

It wasn't true yet, but I'd make it true.

I said, "I'm meeting a friend who'll give us a ride up there tonight." My parents each poured themselves glasses of red wine and nodded and accepted my story the way they accepted all the implausible things I told them to avoid conflict.

I'd started lying to them as a kid—lying at first just to my mother so she wouldn't hit me. But pretty soon I started lying to avoid getting yelled at, too, or to avoid having to talk to her at all. Then I started lying to my stepfather, too, because even though he was tall and kind and used to lift me up in the air with his strong arms, his first loyalty ran to her. The lying became in-stinctive. The mere sight of my mother sent lies shoot-ing off my tongue. I'd blurt whatever popped into my head. *It was a school holiday so I walked downtown and they were giving away free Hello Kitty erasers at the stationery store. No, really, the Mendozas invited me to live with them. They want me to move in right away. I've been accepted to the Beijing Language Institute and I don't need any money. Roberta had an unexpected appointment. And now I'm waiting for a friend to pick me up and take me someplace for college even though I dropped out of high school the first week of junior year.*

"All right," my mother said.

"That's wonderful," my stepfather said. He was bald except for a wispy sprout of gray hair that stuck up from the middle of his head. When my mother wasn't looking, he slipped me one hundred dollars in tens under the table and whispered, "I support you."

It was hardly the thousand tens I was waiting for, but money magnetism, I would learn, is a tricky science.

"Thanks," I whispered.

Later, as my parents watched the *MacNeil Lehrer NewsHour* in their coffin of a bedroom and Maia chewed the foot of my old Curious George doll from when I was a kid, I put on my leather jacket over my sweats, laced up my Doc Martens, and packed our things into the back basket of Maia's blue polka-dot stroller.

I had black jeans and a soft maroon T-shirt. I had the handmade baby sundresses and matching quilt a high school friend who'd recently been born again had sewn for us. I had a flashlight and warm socks. I had a small garnet heart my mother's mother, Gammie Evelyn, gave me that I carried for luck. I had good conditioner, stolen from my mother, and Clinique makeup, also stolen.

I had five books:

The Heart of a Woman by Maya Angelou, which I'd borrowed and failed to return to the Kensington and Chelsea Library a few years earlier and which promised me I could still be a writer even if I was going to be a teenage mother.

for colored girls who have considered suicide / when the rainbow is enuf by Ntozake Shange, which explained some things about men and violence.

The *I Ching*, a regal yellow hardcover I'd always carried, always read the oracle from—sixty-four hexagrams that are said to map our DNA.

Jambalaya by Luisah Teish, a purple hardcover that framed magic as a science of the oppressed.

The Book of Sand by Jorge Luis Borges.

Aim at the horizon, Ariel. That'll be good enough. Sea level. Dirt level. Plan B is the answer, Ariel. They have financial aid at the alternative college up in the North Bay. Lie low. Play dead. Apply to the college.

I opened the door to my parents' dark bedroom, stuck my head in, and said, "My friend's waiting for us. Bye."

They both mewed like cats, and didn't say a word.

Outside, Maia whimpered in the cool night wind as we ambled toward the park where I knew I'd find a comfortable redwood bench. "It's California in August," I whispered into Maia's soft ear. "I love you, but stop whining."

And that was that. Maia puckered her soft baby lips and she never whined again.

I curled up on the wooden park bench with my arms around her the way I used to sleep with my backpack and passport cradled against thieves, and I closed my eyes.

Maybe that night on the park bench, like Borges, I dreamed that my grown-up self was sitting next to us. Maybe in the semiconscious dark, she told me all the wondrous and terrifying things that would happen in the years to come, so that I woke with only a fleeting memory of my dream but with a basic faith that I could answer the questions:

Will we survive?

Can I be a mother and an artist?

Can I be a single mother and a writer?

Can I be a daughter still?

With an unpanicked *Yes. Yes, of course. Follow me.*

In the light of morning, I let the memory of that dream fade. I nursed the baby, buckled her back into her stroller, and we headed for the Caltrain station downtown.

North

Our train started out trainlike, *ch-clack, ch-lack*, and then its train song became a heartbeat, *ch-clack, ch-lack*, became a whisper, hypnotic, *ch-clack, ch-lack*, and the aluminum walls softened and hugged our bodies and we grew with it between molts as our train became an inchworm, became a caterpillar with spiny bristles, hungry, transporting us toward sanctuary. *"Ch-clack, ch-lack,"* I whispered to Maia. *"Ch-clack, ch-lack,"* she suckled back. *Our train, our train, ch-clack, ch-lack.*

Promissory Note

My breast milk leaked through my bra, spreading into giant circles on the front of my T-shirt. My face flushed.

"Sign right here," the financial-aid officer said. She wore pearl earrings, had a dimple in her right cheek.

I'd never not nursed for long enough to leak before. I had Maia with me in her polka-dot stroller, but I hadn't breastfed in the morning session. "I can't go back to orientation like this," I told the woman.

"Don't worry," she said, "an education is the way out of poverty." She was only a couple of years older than me, but when she smiled she reminded me of my Gammie Evelyn and I felt safe. "You won't even notice the loan payments once you get your degree and you get a good job."

She turned a page in her brochure, pointed to a penis-shaped visual aid.

"What's that?"

"It's the graduated repayment program. It rises right along with your career!" She traced rising action with her mauve-manicured index finger. She beamed at Maia asleep in the stroller. "You're making the right choice for your daughter," she said. "Just a couple more places to sign, honey. That's right, honey. Right here."

Magnificent

"You are magnificent," my women's lit professor said. She looked like Susan Sontag, only hotter, and I wanted to gnaw my hand off.

Surely knowing that this is transference will protect me.
  No, knowledge does not protect me.
  Please don't tell me I'm magnificent. Give me even half a reason not to pour all my desire into this transference. Tell me I chose this life, tell me everyone is very embarrassed for me, tell me to aim for the electrical wires. Anything but magnificent.

"No," my women's lit professor laughed, and she threw her head back in the laughing, "I don't say that to just everyone, Ariel. You're absolutely magnificent."

I felt panicky in her presence, but I would not miss class.

I was magnificent.

"You'll have to be a feminist," my Susan Sontag professor said, and she pushed her hair away from her eyes and smiled at me.

I shifted the baby from my left tit to my right. "Why would I be a feminist? Feminists just get abortions."

I grabbed a cloth diaper from the back basket of the stroller, draped it over my shoulder, and repositioned the baby to burp her.

My professor shook her head, glanced down at the syllabus in front of her. "Feminists do what they want." She picked up her coffee mug and brought it to her dark lips. Her nails were painted an easy cream color. She lifted her gaze to look out her office window toward the giant oak tree that shaded the expanse. "Be a feminist," she said. "Do whatever you want."

Out past the oak tree, the September hill sloped to a creek and I knelt at the edge of the water, a flat-chested kid, knobby skinned knees, safe in my body—blood and mud—even as I sat here, too, the baby on my tit, in my professor's office.

And maybe it's true that I was looking at the particular curve of my professor's neck when I said, "Okay."

Rules for Being Twenty

My women's lit professor says I own the language. I can make new words and new stories if the old ones don't suit me. It's how we keep the language alive, she says. I like the way her tongue crests her upper lip when she says *alive*. Alive and thriving.

Don't watch her tongue, Ariel. Just look down. Pretend you think the baby woke up. Pretend you're taking notes.

Tongue to lip.

"Read these," she says, and she pushes two paperbacks across her desk: *Silences* by Tillie Olsen and *Sister Outsider* by Audre Lorde.

Rules for being twenty:

Keep the language alive.

Keep the baby athrive.

Don't let your brain get sucked into the strip mall of suburban motherhood.

If there are only two options, always choose material poverty over psychic poverty.

If there are only two options, create a third option as soon as possible.

The Sonoma County welfare office was an option.

I let the baby play with the bright plastic rings on the cold linoleum floor as I filled out paperwork. I lied here and there on the paperwork. I didn't lie, too. But I always felt like I was lying.

No, I don't get anything beyond tuition in student loan money.

I don't get one hundred dollars a month from my Gammie Evelyn—red envelopes that smell like Paloma Picasso perfume.

No, I don't know where my baby's father lives.

Yes, I have the documentation to prove it: This address on this fake lease. This copy of a check. This state-issued ID. Please just give us our check.

Under the fluorescent lights, women studied their pre-law books. They threatened to slap their crying children. Women checked their watches, their beepers. They chewed blue bubblegum. They filled out paperwork.

Outside, men waited in cars.

I read *Silences* by Tillie Olsen.

A social worker yelled at the mother two spots ahead of me in line. "You lied," she said, and she leaned across the counter, pointed a long, curved fingernail at the woman.

I listened, but I couldn't figure out what lie the lying woman had been caught telling.

Maybe she secretly got one hundred dollars a month from her Gammie Evelyn too.

Maybe there was a man waiting for her in a car outside.

The social worker flashed a silver tooth. "Why did you lie?"

The lying woman adjusted her baby's position on her hip, pulled an older child standing next to her close. "I lied to get the food stamps."

My heart swelled at the honesty of that. *I lied to get the food stamps.*

The social worker squinted and shook her head. "You would lie to get food stamps?"

A woman behind me sucked her teeth. "Like *Thou shall not lie* is one of the goddamn ten commandments?"

The lying woman shrugged at the social worker. "Listen, lady," she said, and she pointed her index finger right back at her. "You'd lie to get food stamps too. If your kids were hungry, you *know* you'd lie."

The social worker shook her head like she didn't know.

She'd lie.

The mother walked away, shaking her head. She put her baby down and let her play with the bright plastic rings on the cold linoleum floor and she redid her paperwork to get back in line.

There were other lies we would learn to tell.

The woman in front of me scurried up to the counter, but just then her toddler started crying loud and she spoke softly and the social worker snapped, "I can't hear you over your kid's tantrum. Back of the line."

I whispered quick in Maia's ear, "We have to be perfect." And we stepped forward.

*

Book response paper: Silences *by Tillie Olsen*
Ariel Gore
Women's Lit 101

Art
Is
All
About
Selling out
Our intimacies.

Motherhood
Is
Just
A silent
Code of silence.

Mothers are the cultural keepers of the lies. *No, he isn't
really an alcoholic. He isn't waiting in the car outside.
This black eye behind my sunglasses is from falling.
I don't know why I keep falling. No, we're not as poor
as you think. See, we have this beautiful, elm-shaded
home and these pretty, unpregnant children. No, we're
not rich either. We're middle class just like we're supposed to be.*

And writers are the cultural tellers of the truth. *This is
what sexuality hurts like. This is the scent of nonjudg-
mental love. This is the texture of a child's hunger. This*

is the sound of sobbing in our middle-class home in the middle of the middle-class night. These are our pink walls, the same color as the sunrise through the plastic bag I thought I would use to suicide.

So it's not just that we haven't had time or money, not just that we haven't found childcare—though we haven't—it's that we're having a hard time reconciling our double roles/double selves.
Hider/exposurist.
Safe-keeper/death-temptress.
Mother/writer.

*

I turned in my paper, hand shaking.
Would my professor still think I was magnificent?

Important Milestones:
Your Baby at Nine Months

May be afraid of strangers
Understands "no"
Puts things in mouth
Pulls to stand
Watches the path of something as it falls

I read the oddly poetic list.

I was still afraid of strangers. And I put things in my mouth.

I lit a cigarette.

Maia watched the path of the smoke as it rose.

Do You Have a Beau?

I hardly talked to anyone I didn't have to, but the voices of the men on the AM radio ranted fast about welfare queens and unfit mothers and all the ways our children would suffer, and the scarlet letter of my bad decisions seared itself into my skin like a brand, reminding me to feel dirty and afraid even when I'd woken up content, my breasts swelling with sustenance.

"At least we know she isn't a lesbian now," my mother's friend Roberta had reassured her amid the horror of my fertility. Roberta had drawn out the *lezzz* so it sounded sharp and strange. *Lezzzbian.*

I ran my shower water scorching hot and scrubbed myself with coarse salt until my skin stung pink.

But shame sticks to skin.

With my student loan money, I'd bought an old Dodge with the radio in it that usually started on the third try and rented a one-bedroom apartment with a muddy little backyard on a cul-de-sac in Petaluma, a suburb maybe forty-five minutes north of San Francisco.

I baked cookies in my oven, feeling like Pippi Longstocking. I bought ten yellow cans of Bustelo coffee, too, and twenty-seven blue packets of rolling tobacco so I wouldn't run out of either until spring semester. I brewed my coffee dark, sipped it until my hands shook, then smoked cigarette after cigarette to make the nervous feeling go away. The tips of my middle and index fingers turned reddish brown from the nicotine. My heart beat fast.

Was the apartment haunted?

Maia watched, silent and attentive, as I burned sage in every room.

I paged through my hardback copy of *Jambalaya* by Luisah Teish and followed her instructions to cleanse the apartment by placing a teaspoon of salt in each corner, moving clockwise from the front door.

I mopped with Van Van floor wash and sprinkled bay rum on the bristles of a broom and beat the walls.

Moving counterclockwise, I picked up the salt and flushed it all down the toilet.

I set the garnet heart from my Gammie Evelyn on the top of a built-in bookshelf, intending to make an altar there.

I lit a blue peace candle and set it on a shelf behind the front door, taped an image of Saint Michael above the doorframe.

I picked five flowers from the bushes at the edge of my muddy yard, placed one in each of five empty jelly jars, and set a jar in each room.

I set a bowl of water next to our double mattress on the floor to keep our dreams clear and I sprinkled lavender under our pillows, but I wasn't sure if all that cleansing could help us now.

Shame is the haunting that's hardest to mop away.

I hardly cared, before the baby, what anyone thought of me, but now I wondered if the men on the AM radio could be onto something. Was my poverty akin to child abuse?

Most nights in that apartment after Maia fell asleep, I stayed up doing economics equations and writing book response papers and stories about straight people without children.

Most nights I secretly waited for Jamie, too, but most nights Jamie didn't show up.

Jamie had been my girlfriend on and off before the baby.

What was she now?

Maybe nothing.

At my round, cigarette-burned dining-room table, I fell asleep on my almost-finished papers, notes scrawled in the margins. At three or four in the morning, I'd wake with a start from a dream about being assaulted by bird-people, and I'd stumble to the mattress where Maia already slept in her soft onesie.

Most nights Jamie never showed up. But occasionally—very occasionally—Jamie knocked on my bedroom window, said "hey" through the gap I left open.

"Hey, Jamie."

Patti Smith sang from the headphones slung around her thin neck.

"Come to the front door," I whispered through the screen.

But when I opened the front door, Jamie looked me up and down and complained, "You're losing weight."

She was one to talk.

She lived in San Francisco.

That city I'd once thought of as my own seemed far away and fancy now.

Jamie told me about the bars people without children went to down there in San Francisco. She told me about Wild Side West and the EndUp. "We play pool," she said. "We have writing groups."

I rolled myself a cigarette, pushed the blue envelope of tobacco across the table toward Jamie, and I imagined the whole world I might live in if I didn't live in my world.

That other world had writing groups. That other world played pool.

Jamie told me about the tattoos people without children got in San Francisco—anchors and butterflies. She showed me a heart with a sword through it on her bicep and I ran my finger along the blade. In San Francisco, a windfall meant roses on your shoulders, meant nautical stars on your elbows. In San Francisco, no one ever had late day-care bills to settle up.

Jamie said they had poetry readings at Red Dora's Bearded Lady Café, and she read me a poem she said was about Gilgamesh—part god, part human—but it was also about all the runaways in a walled city, and the strangeness of that crumbling landscape, and about the way her lover had found the small bones of her shoulders where her wings had broken off.

I tried to ignore the parts of the poem about Jamie's lover.

Maybe she was referring to me?

I didn't think she was referring to me.

I thought maybe she'd brought the poem to tell me something else, something cryptic, but I pushed that thought out of my mind as I pulled thrift-store blankets from my linen closet, made a bed for Jamie and me on my carpeted living-room floor.

I read her a story I'd written and never shown anyone—a story about the way holding the soft and fleshy body of my baby against my chest made me feel married to amazement, but also I guess a story about the way I felt excluded from her walled city where the writers were all runaways and the cafés all red.

Jamie said it was weird to use the word *married* the way I had. She said I should change it to *attached*. But *attached* wasn't quite the right word either, was it? "Bound up?" I tried. "How about *bound up?*"

I was bound up with amazement even if I was losing weight.

Jamie shrugged. She took off her clothes, set the switchblade from her pocket on the windowsill near our bed of blankets, and stretched out.

When I kissed her thigh, she laughed. When I caught her clit between my tongue and my teeth, she shivered. "That's my favorite."

Outside my apartment, it had started to rain.

Jamie. My girlfriend before the baby.

My hand inside her now felt familiar.

But what was she?

I knew the way her breath caught in her jaw just before she came, and I knew that meant to be ready to ease my hand out but keep the pressure on her clit.

What else did I know?

I rested my head on her sharp rib cage as her breath recovered.

In the glow from the streetlights through the window, I watched her breasts rise and fall, but when she noticed me watching, she blushed and covered her nipples with her palms and pulled on a tight bra.

"The lesbians in San Francisco," she whispered, "have cocks."

"Cocks?"

A smile crept across her face. "I brought you one." And from her canvas backpack, Jamie produced a perfect purple silicone phallus. "Do you want me to fuck you?"

Of course I wanted her to fuck me.

I liked the way Jamie pushed her shoulders back as she worked the cock into its leather harness, the way she straightened her spine as she buckled it around her waist. I felt mesmerized as her whole body seemed to morph into something stronger and taller as she stood up with a cock instead of just a cunt.

I knelt in front of her because I wanted her to feel taller still, and I took her cock into my mouth and her ass in my hands, and I liked the way the sounds that came from her throat sounded deeper now.

In college, we read essays about sex and power, but sex and power were for straight people. In college, all the lesbians in all the essays were equals.

"Get on your back," Jamie said.

The two of us had never been equals.

In the glare of morning, a ringing phone woke me. I reached for Jamie, but only found the mess of blankets. I opened my eyes, looked up at the living-room ceiling. No sound from the bedroom where Maia slept. I wrapped a soft sheet around my body, got up to answer the phone.

"Good morning, darling," my Gammie Evelyn breathed.

I sat down at the cigarette-burned table, reached for the tobacco. "Good morning, Gammie," I said. And that's when I saw the note on the table, written in orange ballpoint and paperweighted with an amber rock.

Good morning beautiful Ariel,

You came to me a flame at sunset and I was not accustomed to that soft light.

Like a moth, I fluttered toward you.

Your fire was something I could cover if I tried, but I was afraid I would put you out.

All this to say last night was lovely.

But I also came up here to tell you something. I don't know why I couldn't bring myself to tell you in spoken words, but we're both writers, right? Words on paper are more intimate. You'll still wrap seaweed around my waist, won't you?

I've actually met someone in San Francisco. I wanted you to know. This person, she scares me, but I'm drawn to her intensity.

Call me if you can get a babysitter and come down to San Francisco and maybe meet my girlfriend.

Talk soon and love forever,
Jamie

"Do you have a beau?" my Gammie Evelyn was asking into the phone, and I felt worried because I didn't know how long she'd been asking and how long I'd been silent. I lit my cigarette. My hand smelled like Jamie. "No, Gammie. I don't have a beau."

The morning rain pelted the window.

"That's all right," my Gammie assured me. I could hear her take a drink, and I guessed it was champagne and orange juice at this hour. She usually waited until five o'clock for vodka. She said, "You'll meet a nice beau someday."

And I said, "Thanks, Gammie. Can I call you later?"

As I put the coffee on, I reread Jamie's note, then threw it away. I set the amber paperweight on my altar.

It's not like we were even girlfriends, were we? I wanted to write a note of my own.

Dear Jamie,

Who cares about your fucking sunset metaphors and your slimy-ass seaweed and San Francisco and your pool games and your writing groups and your "someone" and her intensity and your cock?

I mean, seriously? Who fucking cares?

And let's be clear: My light was never something you could cover or put out if you tried. Not ever.

Best of luck with everything that scares you, and have fun in your walled city. I think I won't pay a babysitter to visit it.

　　　　Sincerely,
　　　　Ariel

Maia toddled out from our bedroom. She smiled, all cheeks.

"Morning, baby," I said, my voice more smoker than I thought was cool.

The sun angled through the rainclouds, and the sun said, *Look, it's springtime.*

"We should go outside, baby." I grabbed a little shovel and the packets of seeds I'd been saving.

In our muddy yard, Maia and I planted carrots, broccoli, giant peas, Italian basil, and Greek oregano. I cut my hand with the gardening shovel, but I didn't care. We talked to the seeds, encouraging them to grow strong, grow bound up with amazement, grow fat.

"Grow," I said.

"Go," Maia said, and she painted herself with mud and laughed.

My hand bled, and I laughed too.

Our seedlings sprouted at magic speed and I said, "Good job, keep growing."

Our sprouts shot up and wrapped themselves around us, rooting us to the earth, and Maia said, "Go."

Sometimes, like now, when no one was around but us and time moved however it felt like moving and wrapped its saplings around our legs, I wasn't afraid of anything.

A red-winged blackbird alighted on our wood fence.

I sang up to her from the mud, "What says you, red-winged blackbird?"

"Says you," Maia echoed.

The bird tilted her head to the side like she was surprised at being addressed, and she sang back down to us, "Grow strong, grow bound up with amazement, grow fat!"

I scattered a few seeds in her direction, said, "You're welcome to these, but pretty please don't eat our vegetables unless you have to."

The red-winged blackbird whistled at that and flew down to peck at the seeds and she said, "Isn't it good not to feel afraid?"

BOOK 2
Deepening Action

The Customs of Suburbia

I watched from the front window of our apartment as a young mom with a baby moved into the nice beige house on the other side of the cul-de-sac. She directed movers with her head, whipping her neck around and causing her long hair to wave like a shiny flag, but I didn't hold that against her.

I thought, *We have kids the same age.*

I thought, *We're about the same age.*

I thought, *Maybe we'll be friends.*

But how did people make friends on the cul-de-sac? I didn't know the customs of suburbia, so I made them up. On the following Wednesday morning, I baked banana-chocolate-chip muffins from the *Moosewood Cookbook* and with Maia perched on my hip, I carried the muffins across the street in a napkin-lined basket.

The young mom opened her door and smiled past us. She held her baby on her hip, like me. She took the muffin basket from me, said "thank you," but she didn't invite us inside her nice beige house.

Instead, we talked across the threshold of her doorway.

"Cute little boy," she said toward Maia.

"Oh, she's a girl," I smiled.

The young mom squinted at the blue of Maia's soft flannel shirt and seemed confused, but she didn't say anything more about it. "What does your husband do?" she asked.

"Oh, I'm not married. We moved here last fall. I go to a college outside of town."

Maia looked past the young mom at the toys in their living room. "Ball?"

The young mom sighed and shook her head. "I admire you. I could never go to college. Not while Brittany's little. I couldn't work. We're planning to ho-meschool when she gets older."

Brittany bit her mother's shoulder hard and the woman winced.

I said, "It's work, being home with her—and home-schooling."

"I always wanted to be a stay-at-home mom," the woman said, kind of prying Brittany's jaw from her flesh with her free hand. "I could never leave Britta-ny in day care. Can you imagine letting someone else raise your child?"

"I take Maia to day care sometimes," I admitted, but I knew this wasn't going well. "I can only afford a cou-ple of days a week, but she likes it."

The young mom shook her head. "My gosh," she said. "I don't know how you do it." She took a step back, like she mostly didn't want to know how I did it. She said, "People at our church say that single mothers are selfish and their children should be taken away and put in orphanages, but I think you're amazing. I could never do it all."

I'd heard that before on the AM radio in my car on

the way to school—the thing about single mothers and putting our kids in orphanages—but I didn't really understand it since Maia wasn't an orphan. "We get food stamps and stuff. I'm sure you guys would manage fine."

The young mom smiled past us as she shut her door.

That night in the dim light of our bedroom, I read to Maia from Audre Lorde. I always read to her from whatever I had to read for school. It put her to sleep. I read, "What are the words you do not yet have? What do you need to say? What are the tyrannies you swallow day by day and attempt to make your own, until you will sicken and die of them, still in silence?"

Maia said, "Huney," which meant she was hungry. She said, "Chadee," which meant she wanted to go to the grocery store and push the shopping cart, and she was trying to call the shopping cart a trolley because that's what her father called it when he finally showed up from England, took her to the store, and then said he'd be back in a few months.

Maia liked our multicolored food stamps.

"We'll go to the store and use our food stamps tomorrow, baby."

Maia said, "Nini," which meant she wanted to nurse, and I offered her my tit, so full right then it hurt, and as she latched on and the milk let down, my whole body rushed with the relief of it.

I kept reading to her from Audre Lorde, "Each of us is here now because in one way or another we share a commitment to language and to the power of language, and to the reclaiming of that language which has been made to work against us. In the transformation of silence into language and action, it is vitally necessary for each one of us to establish or examine her function in that transformation and to recognize her role as vital within that transformation."

I wondered what my function could be in that transformation.

How would my role be vital?

*

"Your paper is magnificent," my women's lit professor said, and I hoped she meant she still thought I was magnificent. "But . . ." she said.

My breath caught in my chest.

My professor picked up her coffee mug, looked out her office window toward the giant oak. "There's something to be said for punctuation and grammar. Conventions aren't required, of course, but think of the well-placed comma as elegance."

I liked the way my professor's tongue crested her lip when she said "elegance."

"Elegance?" I asked, but only because I wanted her to say it again.

"Read this," my professor said, and she pushed a paperback across her desk. *Of Woman Born* by Adrienne Rich.

I ran my fingers over the red cover. *Motherhood as Experience and Institution.* I opened to a random page, read a parenthetical: *(the unconscious of the young mother—where does it entrust its messages, when dream-sleep is denied her for years?)* I looked out toward the oak.

I could feel hollow bones and feathery wings push through the muscles of my shoulders, but they didn't break the skin.

That night as I nursed the baby, I read to her from Adrienne Rich, "We have no familiar, ready-made name for a woman who defines herself by choice, neither in relation to children nor to men, who is self-identified, who has chosen herself."

Maia hummed as she fell asleep.

It occurred to me that my mother didn't get a choice about having children. I chose Maia. But I would have to choose myself, too.

I whisper-read, "The nineteenth- and twentieth-century ideal of the mother and children immured together in the home, the specialization of motherhood for women, the separation of the home from the 'man's world' of wage-earning, struggle, ambition, aggression, power, of the 'domestic' from the 'public' or the 'political'—all this is a late-arrived development in human history."

I turned out the light, listened to the sound of Maia's breath in sleep.

Adrienne Rich,

Can I simultaneously be a mother who loves her child and a woman who hates the culture of suburban motherhood?

Can I live in this body, at turns embarrassed and enraged?

What of my dreamless unconscious?

What of the messages I entrust to no one?

What of my unending desire?

I glanced out the window just behind our bed, and here Adrienne Rich sat perched on the roof of a neighbor's garden shed.

I sat up. "Adrienne Rich?"

She had chestnut-colored hair and a goofy smile. "Yes, dear," she whispered through the screen. "Yes to all of your questions, dear. Follow me." And she turned and I watched as black-feathered wings grew from her back. She opened her new wings wide as she leaped into flight and soared off.

Good night, Adrienne Rich.

In the glare of morning, a man yelled outside our apartment, but the man wasn't Maia's father.

The man yelled loud.

Maia cried, "Lauw lauw, Mama." She rubbed her eyes.

The man yelled, "Get out here, you fucking slut!"

I peeled back the curtain to see the man the voice belonged to.

Short, blond hair. He stood next to the green mailbox in our front yard. "Fucking welfare bitch!"

I squinted at him. *Did I know him?*

He wore his Wrangler jeans and white T-shirt tight. "Get out here, you fucking welfare slut. I work and you take welfare?" He flailed his arms. "Come out here with your welfare baby and fight me if you want your welfare so bad."

Was he drunk?

He held something in his hands.

Shit.

An envelope.

"You want your welfare, bitch?"

A woman stood in the street behind him, cried, "Honey, don't."

And, *Oh.* She, I recognized.

The young mom who'd moved into the nice beige house on the other side of the cul-de-sac.

I tried to remember what I might have said to her when I gave her the banana-chocolate-chip muffins, tried to imagine what she might have said to him.

His truck had a bumper sticker that said: GOING THE EXTRA MILE FOR JESUS.

I'd laughed out loud at that when I saw it. Now my heart contracted with fear.

"Come out here and fight me," the man screamed. "Come out here and fight me if you're so *in-de-fucking-pendent.*"

My mouth tasted like copper.

I glanced at Maia, said, "Stay inside, baby," as if *inside* could be our refuge from the man's world.

She stared up at me, didn't answer.

"Just act chill," I whispered.

Outside, I shielded my eyes against the morning, held my open hand out to the man, said, "Give it to me."

He lifted the envelope above his head, held it with both hands, twisted it like he might rip it in half.

Blood rushed to my skin. Our apartment. That check. My only real month's income. I swallowed hard, opened my mouth, "Give me the goddamn check, you asshole."

"What did you call me?" The veins in his neck bulged.

I thought, *Maybe I should have asked nicer.*

"You think I work all day to feed your goddamn welfare baby?"

I clenched my teeth.

"I'd let your baby starve," the man taunted as he stepped back with my check in the envelope. "Take her to an orphanage so good people can raise her."

I clenched my fist. I pulled back and flung the punch, all shoulder—then impact. His cheekbone jutted out like solid glass against my knuckles. I'd never punched anyone in the face before. The sting and the sorrow crashed into my bones.

The young mom behind him shrieked.

The man didn't look hurt, just surprised, as he staggered back.

The woman whimpered. "Please, honey. Don't."

He dropped the envelope onto the pavement between us, said, "I could take you down, bitch, but I don't hit girls." He spat toward the check on the ground, said, "Stay away from my wife."

I didn't say anything.

I bent down.

I picked up the check.

$547 for the month. Almost enough to cover the rent.

The couple watched me from the edge of their lawn.

Maia watched me from the edge of our porch.

What is the word for the blow that doesn't change anything?

*

A mother's job is to keep her children safe.
A writer's job is to make herself vulnerable.
We may have a fundamental conflict here.

*

"It's all right, baby," I said as I climbed the steps. "Let's just go back inside."

"Bit," Maia said, which I'm pretty sure was her attempt at "bitch."

"Bit-POW," I said, and I pumped my fist. I wondered how long my knuckles would ache.

Maia grinned, made a tiny fist. "Bit-POW," she said. "Mama bit-POW."

And I tried to smile at that. "Mama bit-pow."

*

As Maia nursed that night, her brown eyes open, I read to her from Adrienne Rich: "Misogyny is not a projection of women who resent men."

She released her mouth grip from my tit and said, "Genie," which I think was what she heard when I said "misogyny."

I read, "I know no woman—virgin, mother, lesbian, married, celibate—whether she earns her keep as a housewife, a cocktail waitress, or a scanner of brain waves—for whom her body is not a fundamental problem: its clouded meaning, its fertility, its desire, its so-called frigidity, its bloody speech, its silences, its changes and mutilations, its rapes and ripenings."

As Maia's eyes fluttered shut, I whispered from the book, "To seek visions, to dream dreams, is essential, and it is also essential to try new ways of living, to make room for serious experimentation, to respect the effort even where it fails."

To Protect Yourself from a Neighbor

If you suspect a neighbor of giving you the evil eye, place a small mirror on the windowsill facing their home and whisper, "Return to sender."

Check Cashing

I brought the welfare check to Capitalist Bank, said hello to the teller as I set it down with the deposit slip.

She picked up the blue check by its edges, like it might have cooties. She turned it over, and then over again. She scooted her glasses up on her nose, looked at the computer screen next to her. "I'm sorry, miss," she said. "Your bank account has been closed."

"What do you mean, closed?" I'd had an account at Capitalist Bank since I was seven years old and got my first paper route by lying to the newspaperman that I was already ten. My signature card still had the backward *R*s on it. I said, "Can we reopen it?"

The teller pursed her lips. "I'm sorry, miss," she said. "Once we close an account, it's closed. There's a check-cashing place on the other side of the river."

I looked around the branch at the other white people going about their business. They signed checks and filled out deposit slips and withdrawal slips. Behind desks, they typed things into computers. They examined their own manicures. They looked up at the clock. They counted their cash. They didn't seem to notice me. I couldn't blame them. When I had been them, I didn't notice me either.

I thought everyone could have a bank account.

I pushed the door open with my hip, maneuvered the stroller outside.

"This bank sucks," I said to Maia.

"Sucks," she said softly.

I walked fast, pushing the stroller toward the concrete bridge and over it, across the river and into the glass office with the neon sign that flashed CHECKS CASHED.

Here in yellowish light, the workers of Petaluma stood in line—the farm laborers holding their gloves and the mothers pushing strollers and the construction guys with their tool belts and the teenagers in fast-food uniforms. A sign on the wall read,

FEES
Government checks: Greater of $10 or 10%
Personal checks: Greater of $20 or 20%
Seven-day hold on checks over $1,000

And then in much smaller letters: *Owned and Operated by Capitalist Bank.*

I did the math. They'd charge me more than fifty dollars for the welfare check and twenty dollars more for the check from my Gammie Evelyn.

The man standing next to me must have noticed my mouth as it began to form an *O*. His hands were large and calloused. "It's expensive to be poor," he laughed.

I wanted to laugh too, but I was thinking about my rent as I waited my turn to push my checks under the glass.

Lamb's Tongue

"Jesus Christ, Ariel. This is the baby's library?" My mother tossed through books. "You can't read Adrienne Rich to the baby. You'll scare her." She lifted Maia up from the carpet and marched her outside, buckled her into the car seat in the back of her old maroon Volvo, and drove off.

I made coffee, wrote book response papers at the dining-room table, read Rob Brezsny's *Real Astrology* in the local weekly paper:

This is how spells are broken . . .
By burning down the dream house
where your childhood keeps repeating itself.

I drew a picture of my childhood dream house on butcher paper and burned it in the kitchen sink.

Sunny midafternoon and my mother and Maia came home carrying a witch doll from the folk arts store, organic bubble bath from the co-op, and a large hardback reproduction of the original 1812 Brothers Grimm version of "Rapunzel" as it appeared in *Children's and Household Tales* from the antiquarian bookstore.

I fed my mother and Maia carrot sticks and lentils we'd bought with my food stamps. Maia showed her nona the Speak & Spell toy we'd picked up at the Goodwill, and I noticed she had a witchy gleam in her brown eyes when she pushed the buttons.

"M. M. M."

I paged through the book appropriate for children.

Once upon a time a married couple who longed for a baby finally conceived, but pregnancy brought with it irrational cravings.

From the small rear window of her house, the pregnant woman could see into her neighbor's magical garden that bloomed with flowers, herbs, and vegetables. The pregnant woman fixated on the lamb's lettuce, also called "rapunzel," that grew in one of the raised beds near the edge of the garden.

Everyone in town knew that neighbor was a witch who'd somehow managed to survive the burning years in Europe. The last witches had just been put to death in Prussia and Switzerland, but it still would have been social suicide for the pregnant woman to knock on the witch's door and ask her for some of that lamb's lettuce—so rich in vitamins C, E, and B9, as well as beta-carotene and essential fatty acids. How could she get that lamb's lettuce? The pregnant woman had to have it. "Oh," she cried to her husband, swooning her hand to her forehead like she might faint. "If I don't get some rapunzel from the garden behind our house, I shall surely die!"

The man loved his wife, and he feared her irrationality. Yes, he would get her some of that lamb's lettuce—which was also called "lamb's tongue." He would get it for her whatever the cost. He pulled on his boots, climbed over the high wall, dug up a handful of the greens, and dashed home to make salad. And, *oh*, that salad was good—nutty and tangy, with just the right hint of bitterness.

The pregnant woman devoured it, and licked her fingers, but she wasn't satisfied. "I must have more of that lamb's tongue."

The man saw there would be no peace. He put on his boots again. He climbed the wall again. But this time when he landed in the witch's garden, she stood right in front of him with her hands on her hips. "Oh, Frau Gothel," the man stuttered. "Forgive me. My wife is finally pregnant. Surely it would be dangerous to deny her anything."

The witch sucked her teeth. "*Now* you know my name?" She crossed her arms and pursed her lips. "But instead of knocking on my door and asking for some of my lettuce, you decided to scale the back wall like a raccoon?"

"Please," the man begged, down on his knees now.

The witch shook her head. "It's fine. Take as much rapunzel as you like. But the two of you aren't the only ones who can have irrational desires and lay claim to things not your own. That baby belongs to me. Enjoy your salad."

"Of course, of course," the man whimpered. "Thank you for your lenience."

And so it was that when the pregnant woman gave birth to that planned child in a two-parent household, the witch appeared, named the little girl Rapunzel, and took her away.

In the abundance of the witch's garden, Rapunzel grew up fat and nourished, but the witch herself remained flawed and conflicted. She'd lived so many years ostracized from her community and she didn't miss the solitude. Maybe she felt unworthy, having scammed custody of Rapunzel the way she did over a few heads of stolen lamb's tongues. If she were to be honest, she would admit that she feared abandonment. And even though she'd been a witch all her life, female sexuality still confused her. So it was that when Rapunzel turned twelve and the witch could see that her little girl wasn't the knobby-kneed child playing at the creek's edge anymore, she led Rapunzel into a high tower that had neither door nor stairway—just a little window at the very top—and she locked Rapunzel inside and she axed the ladder into kindling.

When the witch wanted to see her daughter, she stood below and called up:

Rapunzel, Rapunzel!

Let down your hair.

And Rapunzel had Stockholm syndrome, so of course she let down her hair. And, *oh*, Rapunzel had the most beautiful hair. Rapunzel untied it, wound it around a window hook, watched it fall the twenty yards to the ground.

What does it feel like when your mother climbs your hair like it's a ladder? The pain rips at your scalp. You struggle to breathe.

But Rapunzel was imbued with a survival magic no one quite understood and, miraculously, the weight of her mother didn't snap her neck.

Time passed, as they say in fairy tales, in lieu of a transition, and one day a young prince happened through the forest where the tower stood and he saw beautiful Rapunzel up at her window, singing, and he fell instantly in love. He looked for a door to the tower where he might let himself in, but found none. It didn't occur to him to call up to Rapunzel, to learn her name, to compliment her singing voice, or to ask her if there was anything he could do to help liberate her from her obvious imprisonment.

The prince just wanted to figure out how to get up there. So he decided to stalk Rapunzel, which wasn't that difficult given her predicament.

Every day, he came to the forest and secretly spied on her.

Finally, he saw the witch, who approached the tower and called out,

Rapunzel, Rapunzel!

Let down your hair.

Ah, now he knew how to get into the tower of female sexuality.

The next day, as soon as it was dark, he went to the tower and called up,

Rapunzel, Rapunzel!

Let down your hair.

And she did.

Rapunzel gasped at the sight of the strange man who climbed her hair, but the prince sang that Simon &

Garfunkel song about Mrs. Robinson, which charmed her, and female desire is real and can't be locked in a tower, and soon Rapunzel came to like the prince so well that she arranged for a daily booty call, and thus, according to the Brothers Grimm, Rapunzel and the prince lived in "secret joy and pleasure for a long time."

The witch, not particularly intuitive, was none the wiser until Rapunzel wondered out loud, "Tell me why it is that my clothes are all too tight. They no longer fit me."

"You slut!" the witch cursed. "What am I hearing from you? Everyone will be very embarrassed for you." She grabbed her daughter's hair, wrapped it around her left hand a few times, grabbed a pair of scissors, and—*snip snip*—cut it off. The witch kept her daughter's hair, but threw Rapunzel out into the wilderness with nothing but the clothes on her back and the new pixie haircut.

Rapunzel felt alone and afraid that first night as she slept on a park bench, but she savored her freedom. She hiked and she wandered, she foraged and she gave birth to twins unassisted.

No one cut her.

Back at the tower, the witch tied Rapunzel's hair to the window hook and waited.

When the prince called out,
Rapunzel, Rapunzel!
Let down your hair.
The witch let down the hair.

In the wilderness, Rapunzel marveled at how good her

scalp felt. She ran her fingers through her short locks, rubbed her healing skin with rosemary oil. She nourished herself with wild lamb's tongue and nursed her children.

At the top of the ladder of golden hair, the prince startled to find the witch instead of his newly knocked-up girlfriend.

"You little creep," the witch scoffed at him. "Now we've both lost her."

The prince, who also couldn't deal with abandonment, flung himself from the tower, but survived—blinding his eyes in a rose bush as he crashed down.

Time passed. The prince wandered the forest weeping and eating nothing but grass and roots.

At last, he happened upon a mother and her children. They were vegan like him, and he thought the mother's voice sounded familiar.

Rapunzel recognized the prince immediately, and in her loneliness, she threw her arms around his neck and cried, and even though she was a slutty teenage single mother, her tears held a magic, and as they fell into the prince's eyes, they brought sight back to the whole world of blind male entitlement.

The End

Blood-Red Bougainvillea

The phone rang in the dark—my ex-boyfriend. Lance. The baby's father. He'd moved to town for real this time, he said.

"Good news," he laughed into the phone. "Good news and a hundred bucks." He started singing that Clash song about your daddy being a bank robber, and I shrugged into it.

He'd found a live-in job taking care of a dying woman who collected ceramic angels and plastic troll dolls with neon-colored hair. Part of his job was to arrange the angels and the trolls into makeshift social clusters on the low tables around the woman's home hospital bed.

On his morning breaks, he brought us applesauce and printer paper.

Maia reached for him. "Dada?"

I made Bustelo coffee in my sunlit corridor of a kitchen, Jimmy Cliff on the cassette player. I liked Lance well enough in the mornings when he was easy, but I kept my hands free for quick blocking because I knew he could turn violent on a dime and two shots of whiskey.

At night, he yelled on my front porch.

I bought a dead bolt at Rex Hardware on Fourth Street and B and installed it, but Lance just smashed the glass panes of the door, his blood dripping onto my beige renter's carpet inside as he unlocked it.

"Can I stop over tonight?" he asked on the phone now. "I got a hundred bucks."

I knew it didn't matter if I said yes or no, but for the record, I said, "Yes." I said, "Sure." And maybe that's the part I shouldn't tell you: as often as I tried to lock it out, I invited male violence into our home.

I invited it in, again and again.

I felt sorry for it, I guess.

Poor little angry, hurt boy left out in the cold.

Poor little male violence.

You can climb my hair.

I could certainly use the one hundred dollars, even if I knew it would only be thirty-seven dollars by the time he got here. He'd bring a full pack of cigarettes too. Cigarettes and thirty-seven dollars.

*

The phone rang in the dark—my girlfriend. Well, my ex-girlfriend now. Jamie.

She was calling from a pay phone on Mission Street in San Francisco, her voice an echo. "The vultures are circling," she whispered. I couldn't tell if she was high or just spooked. "A whole wake of them ready to swoop down and feed on me."

Her new girlfriend was threatening to kill herself.

"I can't handle another death," Jamie cried, "She'll throw herself off the Golden Gate Bridge if I leave. It's gonna be all my fault."

She'd already jumped from the rooftop of their college, the girlfriend, but she'd only broken a few bones. She was HIV positive, the girlfriend, but that's not why Jamie wanted to leave. "Should I leave?" she kept asking.

I didn't know.

The *I Ching* told her to wait, to be yielding and receptive.

"I can't leave," Jamie said.

I was starting to kind of hate the *I Ching*.

"Remember Spain?" Jamie whispered.

The squat outside Valencia where I'd lived with Jamie and Lance before the baby seemed very far away now, like a book we'd once read—its images bathed in the candle-lit romance that illuminates the memory of hunger but not the hunger itself.

I sat on my blood-stained beige renter's carpet, surveyed the fairy-tale books and sock-monkey stuffed animals and Speak & Spell and the witch doll as Jamie went quiet.

I picked up a ballpoint pen, wrote on the edge of a diaper: *Maybe you don't have to have a baby to sink into silences.*

A siren down Mission Street.

"Maybe I should be the one to kill myself," Jamie said softly.

And I wondered why female violence was always so quick to turn on itself.

Like, *Stay the hell away from me, female violence.*
I completely deny you, female violence.
Take one more step and I will kill you, female violence.
No, seriously, you're dead to me.
I will kill myself.
A click and Jamie was gone.

*

The phone rang in the dark—my Gammie Evelyn, who sent me one hundred dollars a month in red envelopes. "Darling," she breathed into the phone. "I'm just calling to tell you how marvelous you are."

I imagined my Gammie on the other end of the phone, her gray hair piled into a bun, a red silk scarf tied around it, her red manicured nails clutching a vodka tonic. Her skin was slightly darker than the rest of the women in our family, so she always joked about the milkman. "I can't stand it," she sighed. "I'm the last Democrat in Orange County."

I held the receiver away from my mouth so my Gammie wouldn't hear the inhale and exhale of my cigarette.

"Darling," she said. "You're doing a marvelous job—as well as anyone could do—but children need fathers, don't you agree?"

I could hear Frank Sinatra singing "I Gotta Be Me" in the background.

I opened my palm and crushed my cigarette into

the center because that hurt in just the right way. I pressed it harder. The smell of burning flesh.

"I didn't always have a father," I said.

I remembered waking, maybe two years old, and smoothing the satin trim of my soft pink blankie between my fingers. I remembered the blood-red bougainvillea that vined and bloomed just outside the open window. My mother and my father and I had been living in France. That's when my father went fully batshit and locked us all in a white-walled apartment and nobody will tell me what went down next, but after that it's the French police breaking down the door and escorting my mother and me out into the rain, and after that it's a cold airplane and "Go to sleep, Ariel," and we land back in my Gammie Evelyn's orange-wallpapered guest bedroom in Southern California, like safe.

"Well, that was awful," my Gammie sighed into the phone now.

As I hung up, I wondered if she was right about children needing fathers. I mean, how would I know? I loved my father, but the logistics of food on the table weren't really in his skill set.

*

A knock at the door and I stood up slowly, padded across the stained beige carpet, unbolted the lock so that Lance wouldn't have to smash another windowpane.

He smiled as he stepped inside, started singing that Clash song "London Calling" as he opened a full pack of cigarettes and held it out to me.

"Thanks," I said. I took a cigarette, brought it to my lips, lit it, and inhaled. The smoke felt warm in my lungs, like comfort—familiar and deadly.

I exhaled, measuring my breath into an imagined future in which I might more marvelously control what I let in and what I expelled.

Things That Are Red
Besides the Scarlet Letter

Blood

My Gammie Evelyn's Cadillac

My mother's fingernails

Passion

Cherries

Red Dye No. 2, which we weren't allowed to eat
when we were kids

Fire

The devil

The apple from the tree of knowledge

Also, the poison apple the witch gives to Snow
White

Seduction

Pomegranates

Bolshevik utopia

Hot sauce

The Red Sea, the crossing of which in alchemical
symbolism refers to the most difficult stage in a
person's life

Shame

Insects crushed into dye

Stop signs

Hot peppers

The first color a brain-injury patient can perceive after temporary color blindness

The shoes that get Dorothy home

Anger

Miscarriage

Fever

Rash

Carpets for important and glamorous people

Sex-worker districts

The sunrise

Sunset

Rising stock markets (in Asian symbolism)

Falling stock markets (in North American symbolism)

The color European settlers associated with Native American skin

Burns

Scars

Stretch marks

In linguistic history, the first color after black and white—meaning that all languages have words for black and white. If a third color word exists, it's red.

Our Skin Is Alive with Signals

I shaved my legs with a dull razor, slathered on lotion I'd found in the clearance bin at the pharmacy on Petaluma Boulevard, imagined I could make my skin soft and smooth like the girls in magazines.

I weighed 125 pounds. I smoked cigarettes for breakfast. I ate just enough to keep my breasts full of milk for the baby. Four ounces of ground turkey cost less than a dollar, 130 calories, twenty-six grams of protein. If I only used the calories to make breast milk, they didn't count.

I read to Maia from Adrienne Rich: "We are neither 'inner' nor 'outer' constructed; our skin is alive with signals; our lives and our deaths are inseparable from the release or blockage of our thinking bodies."

I'd thought I'd made all this upward progress toward my own unsilencing freshman year, but now I felt the shame descending to cloak my skin again and I didn't know why. I wanted my arc to keep rising.

Our skin.
My skin.
Our thinking bodies.

Some nights I woke in a strobe-light kind of a panic.

Had something happened to the baby? My own mortality, too, made my veins sting with anxiety. If something happened to me, where would that leave her?

Violent homes.

Specter of orphanages.

Maybe this single mom thing *was* irresponsible.

I didn't want her to live with Lance and the dying lady with the troll dolls.

I didn't want my mother to take her.

I typed stories and xeroxed them and folded them into legal-sized envelopes and sent them off to all the literary journals—*CALYX* and *Glimmer Train* and the *Paris Review*—always including a Self-Addressed Stamped Envelope for the replies. The rejections came back, always short on postage and always addressed in my own shaky handwriting. When I saw the way I'd written *Ariel Gore* on the envelope, I knew my story wasn't wanted. It was like I was rejecting myself. Over and over, I rejected myself.

I weighed 120 pounds. I smoked cigarettes for lunch. The rice and curry they served in the college cafeteria was only for the kids who lived on campus. Mothers and children weren't allowed to live on campus. A bag of spinach in the expired pile at the co-op cost less than a dollar, twenty-eight calories, 668 milligrams of potassium, 224 percent of the daily recommended supply of vitamin A.

Maia would have perfect eyesight.

I'd stay up late on the computer, scorching mine.

I read to her from Audre Lorde: "To search for power within myself means I must be willing to move through being afraid to whatever lies beyond."

I felt afraid.

I wrote stories no one read. My skin didn't look like the skin of the girls in magazines.

I weighed 117 pounds. I smoked cigarettes for dinner. The coffee had no calories. Maybe now I was in control. If I was the one to decide I was unworthy of nutrition, maybe I could get the power back.

I needed the power back.

God, how can I get the power back?

The baby kept growing.

I needed the power back.

Maia played with her Speak & Spell from the Goodwill, pushed random buttons. The electronic voice said, "Spell *raven*."

She pushed buttons. "B. X. P."

"Incorrect. Spell *raven*."

"Z. E. Z."

The electronic voice said, "That is incorrect. The correct spelling of raven is R-I-B-B-O-N."

Oh, ribbon, I realized. But it didn't matter. Maia just pushed buttons.

I started to roll a cigarette, then thought I heard a faint moaning sound coming from our backyard. I peered out the window and squinted. A woman writhed in the mud. *Was she naked?* I opened the door. "Can I help you?"

The woman looked up at me, her breasts covered in mud, her face covered in mud. She moved her head fast and her muddy hair whipped around like a flag and now I recognized her: the young mom from the nice beige house on the other side of the cul-de-sac.

"Are you all right?" I realized I didn't even know her name.

She made a low chirping sound as she shoved barely ripe peas into her mouth, pulled barely ripe carrots from the earth.

Was she off her medication?

She stood up and spun around.

"What are you doing?" I asked.

"I don't know," the woman half cried as she kept turning.

I rubbed my forehead hard. I couldn't very well leave her out there in the mud having whatever kind of breakdown she was having, but what if I helped her and she sold me out to her husband again and this time he might decide that he did, in fact, hit girls? I said, "Where's your baby?"

The woman cried.

I said, "Is your husband home?"

And she shook her head and rubbed mud into her hair.

"Is Brittany at home?" I asked, my voice edging into panic.

But the young mom didn't answer me.

I padded back into my apartment fast, picked up Maia with her Speak & Spell.

"Spell *skin*," the electronic voice commanded.

We walked fast across the street, the pavement cold under my bare feet.

The door to the nice beige house stood open.

"Brittany?" I called inside.

Maia pushed buttons. "Y. O. Y."

"Incorrect. Spell *skin*."

"Y. Y. Z."

Brittany sat wide-eyed alone on the green shag carpet, her white nightgown smeared with baby food.

"C'mon," I said, and I picked her up onto my free hip, my heart beating like a trapped bird in my chest imagining everything that could go wrong if the woman's husband or anyone else arrived right now and wanted to know what I was doing there grabbing this baby I barely knew, but no one arrived.

"That is incorrect. The correct spelling of *skin* is S-P-I-N."

At home, I let the babies play with pots and pans as I coaxed the woman out of the mud and into the shower. I noticed that her skin was soft like the girls in magazines. After I'd dressed her in an old T-shirt of mine and sweats, she sat shivering at my cigarette-burned dining-room table, begging me, "Just please don't tell my husband."

I set a mug of hot tea in front of her.

"Woman to woman," she whined. "Promise me that much?"

My heart swelled with compassion for the young mom who lived in the nice beige house on the other side of the cul-de-sac, but I felt irritated too. I said,

"You know, I haven't slept in a long time either." I rolled myself a cigarette. I sipped tea and savored the hot as it eased down my scorched throat. I held the warm mug in my hands. I said, "Our skin is alive with symbols."

The woman sat up straight, like she'd suddenly remembered who she was and where. She pursed her lips and her eyes darted past me. "I have no idea what you're talking about."

From the living room, I could hear the clang of pans and the electronic voice that spoke to our daughters. "Spell *wander.*"

"P. G. R."

"Incorrect. Spell *wander.*"

The woman from the nice beige house on the other side of the cul-de-sac cleared her throat. "I think I should go."

"H. H. K."

"That is incorrect. The correct spelling of *wander* is W-O-N-D-E-R."

I didn't show the woman out. I just listened as she picked up her baby and opened and closed the door behind her.

Was it me, or were people remarkably weird?

"Spell *anger.*"

"T. T. T."

"Incorrect. Spell *anger.*"

"T. T. T."

"That is incorrect."

On the back of an envelope, I made a shopping list in red crayon: *tomatoes, peppers, beets, radishes, snapper, kidney beans, cayenne, apples, blood oranges.* I wasn't old enough to buy wine yet, but I tacked it onto the end of the list anyway. Usually with the baby, no one carded me. *Red wine.*

I called to Maia in the living room, "Let's go to the grocery store with our food stamps, baby."

And she called back, "Chadee?"

Overcoming

Write what you know, my women's lit professor kept saying, but what I knew wasn't shaped like a story and now I was a sophomore and I needed to write an underground feminist classic.

AIM HIGH, the Everest poster in that junior college career counselor's office said. Stories always climbed upward. *I mean, what's the point if your experience isn't inspirational?* But at twenty-one, all I wanted was to be a mother and an artist and not commit suicide—not exactly inspirational.

What could I write about overcoming?

I wasn't overcoming. I was just smoking a lot and getting by.

Some days I felt stronger and I talked with egrets and cypresses—I asked them whether it was better to be migratory or rooted—but most nights I froze with panic. *What was I doing?* The only alternative to a mountaintop story, it seemed, was to become a cautionary tale. Maybe I could write a monumentally pitiful piece about all the ways I'd really fucked up my life and if people read it they'd learn from my mistakes and they'd stay in high school, dammit, and they wouldn't wander around the world and they wouldn't smoke hash and they wouldn't get mired in the mess of their own sexuality and they wouldn't get pregnant and they wouldn't have children and everything for them would be fine—they would become the happy ending I could never be.

So in a way, still the overcoming.

I'll tell you a story of overcoming.

It isn't my story.

It's a true story of overcoming.

Well, it's a *mostly* true story of overcoming.

Close your eyes. Picture Paris in the early 1860s with its stone arches and narrow alleys and waterways that all smelled of rot. The Eiffel Tower hasn't yet been erected, but the spire of Notre Dame points upward.

It's here in the heat of late summer that Augustine Gleizes, the girl-child of domestic servants, emerged into a world built for rising action.

Augustine lived with a wet nurse her first nine months, then with relatives. That's how working parents did things then. When she was finally old enough to go to school, her family sent her to a convent east of the city.

A charming kid with a quick smile, Augustine wanted what all kids want: to be fed, to be accepted, to be loved, to be protected. She laughed and she prayed. She hoped to fit in. She got bored. She teased the nuns. She got caught masturbating. The nuns tied her hands down at night so she wouldn't touch herself. When that didn't work, they slapped her. They put her in an isolation cell. They threw holy water in her face. They decided she was possessed. They beat her and told her their violence would exorcise her demons. She kept masturbating.

In the afternoons, she took walks in the countryside.

She let the local boys kiss her in exchange for candy. She made a woman-friend in town, and watched as her friend's husband hit her and kicked her and dragged her by the hair.

What's it always with the hair?

These were Augustine's first lessons in becoming female.

Imagine Augustine's relief when she turned thirteen and her mother finally showed up and told her it was time to come home and learn to sew alongside their boss's kids.

Home they went together, mother and daughter, Augustine smiling hopeful as she thought of all the pretty red dresses she might make.

Augustine's new bedroom wasn't exactly a bedroom—more like a closet under the stairs—but she tried to be a good sport about it. She soon realized she had a bigger problem anyway. Her parents' boss propositioned Augustine when his wife was away. She turned him down, but he insisted that she move into his room and sleep in his bed anyway. He said he'd buy her beautiful things if she'd just give herself to him. When she said no again, he pretended to respect her wishes, but that night he held a razor to her throat and he raped her.

Thirteen years old.

That's when Augustine seriously lost her shit.

She stayed in bed. She couldn't walk. A doctor who didn't examine her dismissed her complaints as a first period instead of the injuries of rape.

But she didn't just have cramps. She had panic attacks and convulsions. On an errand in town, she ran into the boss on the street. He grabbed her hair and threatened her. She had nightmares. She hallucinated eyes looking at her during the day. She had bouts when her body felt numb, her gut hurt, when she couldn't breathe or move her limbs. Sometimes she seemed all right—the charming laugh, the quick flirt. But then again with the fits. She'd fall to her knees and pray, laugh uncontrollably, then weep.

Her parents found her a job as a chambermaid in another house—maybe another house would make things all right—but on her days off she hung out with her brother, smoked cigarettes, and started sleeping with her brother's friends. When one boy got jealous of another, the jealous one tattled on slutty Augustine, and her parents, enraged, brought her home. In the arguing uproar about their shameful teenage daughter that night, Augustine learned her family's secrets:

1. Her brother was not her father's son.
2. Her mother was the boss's lover. (Did that mean her brother was her rapist's son?)
3. Her mother knew from the start that Augustine would never learn to sew and sing with the boss's kids. Augustine's mother had knowingly sold her to the boss for sex.

Augustine screamed, couldn't stop screaming. Her body convulsed in pain and terror. She screamed until the right side of her body stiffened into paralysis.

Her mother didn't know what to do with her. She paced in guilt and self-centered panic. She took Augustine to a children's hospital for epilepsy, but the doctors said she wasn't epileptic. So it was that, on October 21, 1875, when Augustine had just turned fourteen, her mother took her to the Pitié-Salpêtrière Hospital in Paris, a warehouse asylum for female indigents, and permanently committed her.

An asylum can be a tower.

The hospital's first notes about Augustine make her sound like any fourteen-year-old who's been bounced around: "Active, intelligent, affectionate, impressionable, and capricious. She loves being the center of attention."

Based on the amount of time she spent on her hair, doctors decided that "everything in her announced the hysteric." So they prodded her and needled her like a lab rat. They examined her eyelids and her nostrils, examined her tongue, and pressed into her vagina until her body started to shake. They said her right side was weaker than her left, they watched her pull away and convulse. They cataloged her symptoms while she screamed at them, "What do you know about medicine? I don't want you anywhere near me!"

But the doctors didn't back off.

Augustine screamed, "Take that snake out of your trousers."

She fascinated them.

She screamed, "No, I won't uncross my legs! Let me go."

But the doctors didn't let Augustine go.

Instead, they took her picture in the hospital photography studio.

Remarkable!
Strangely beautiful!
They took photograph after photograph. Maybe with the sound of one of the clicks, something inside of Augustine snapped open. She arched her back. *Click click.* She fell into prayer. *Click click.* She laughed until she cried. *Click click.* She laughed until she bled. *Click click.* Her blouse fell open. *Click click click.* Her breakdown edged into performance.

Excited by her condition, her doctor introduced her to his class, saying, "One of the patients in our service, afflicted with hysteron-epilepsy, has developed a rare pathological condition that as such is worthy of being placed before your eyes. It is by nature essentially unstable and mobile, as is the sex it prefers to afflict."

Did violence prefer to afflict the female body?

They called Augustine the "queen of the hysterics." *Click click.*
   She made her doctors stars. *Click click.*
   Oh, arch your back again like that, won't you, Augustine?
   She reenacted her own rape, screaming as her body convulsed, "Pig! Pig! I'll tell Papa, pig! You're so heavy! You're hurting me!"
   Do it again, Augustine.
   "He put rats in my behind! You're a despicable mother!"
   This time we'll hypnotize you on stage.
   "No," Augustine finally screamed, exhausted.

But she was a celebrity now. She was a career maker. The doctors needed her.

Do it, Augustine. Or we'll put you in solitary confinement.

"What do you know about medicine? I don't want you anywhere near me."

Uncross your legs, Augustine.

But Augustine didn't uncross her legs. She fell into prayer, pretended to fall asleep, cried and laughed.

During a lecture, Augustine wouldn't shut up. Her doctor induced an "artificial contraction" of her tongue and larynx, and she went silent. She was sent back to the ward mute. *Yes, violence seemed to prefer to afflict the female body.* When Augustine finally recovered her voice, her symptoms vanished.

Nothing left to do with her now that she wouldn't perform, her doctors gave her a job as a ward girl. They called her in and hypnotized her when they felt like it, photographed her in her uniform. They prodded and needled her, finally succeeded in causing a relapse.

She convulsed and yelled.

The doctors put her in a straitjacket.

She tore the jacket, smashed a window, and hid a huge shard of glass under her mattress.

They put her in a cell.

After two months of isolation, she managed to break a bracket from the casement window in her cell and escape.

The next day she was found sitting in a cold bath.

Doctors returned her to the ward but, mercifully, not to her cell.

Her doctor tried to hypnotize her one more time, but Augustine wouldn't have it.

She tried to escape, got caught, and tried again.

Under her old mattress, she found her hidden shard of glass.

Maybe this could be her escape.

Augustine cut off her own hair and watched the locks as they fell to the floor. She crept through the dark hospital. She knew where an intern kept a spare set of clothes. She changed quickly, and she walked out of the Pitié-Salpêtrière Hospital with a smooth swagger like she knew exactly where she was going. The guards glanced up as she passed them, but those guards didn't blink at the man they saw. Augustine slipped into the Parisian night—twenty years old and a free person.

And no one ever heard of Augustine Gleizes again.

That's a story of overcoming.

With her famous face, how did Augustine elude recognition?

She probably just kept her suit and hat on.

Maybe she became your great grandfather.

Or mine.

The One That Got Away

My phone rang in the dark.

"Ariel?" The urgency in my mother's voice made me straighten my spine.

"Yes?" *Had someone died?*

"I know you think you're a lesbian, Ariel," my mother said gravely. "But I've found the perfect man for you."

I sat down at my round table and, in the pink glow from the streetlight outside, started to roll a cigarette.

"Tiniest," my mother said, "I know you've had some bad experiences with men, but that doesn't mean the right one isn't out there. You're not *that* ugly."

I wasn't *that* ugly? I lit the cigarette. I never knew if my mother was kidding or what.

My mother said, "Tiniest, he's perfect. He's from the Midwest. He's a Taurus. He's overweight."

"Sounds like exactly my type." The cigarette smoke felt hot in my lungs. I practiced blowing it out my nose.

She said, "Tiniest, he's a journalist just like you want to be. And he's funny. I'm telling you, he's perfect for you. I'm sure he won't mind you already have a baby. Like I said, he's overweight."

I started rolling another cigarette even though I hadn't finished the first one.

"Are you listening to me, Tiniest?"

I lit the second cigarette off the cherry of the first. "Yes, Mom. I'm listening."

My mother said, "His name is Michael Moore. He's made a film called *Roger & Me*. He's giving a talk at Stanford on Friday. Why don't you and the baby come down? John can watch the baby and you and I will go to the lecture, and there will certainly be a reception afterward where we can meet him. He's right in your league. You can get him."

"Get him?" I crushed the cigarette into my forearm.

The streetlight outside flickered and the moon winked at me.

My mother sighed. "He's sixteen years older than you are, Tiniest. I know that, but that still makes him younger than Lance. Just see if you can lighten your hair a little before Friday and come down."

"Lighten my hair?"

My mother cleared her throat.

I thought I could hear Pink Floyd in the background.

She said, "Tiniest, he's the perfect man. If you *do* decide to become a lesbian, my *only* revenge will be to know that you'll spend the *rest* of your life knowing that you could have had Michael Moore if you'd only listened to your mother."

If I'd only listened to my mother.

*

I crept into the bedroom, Maia already asleep on our mattress. I read aloud to myself from Audre Lorde's

Sister Outsider in the moonlight: "When we live outside ourselves, and by that I mean on external directives only rather than from our internal knowledge and needs, when we live away from those erotic guides from within ourselves, then our lives are limited by external and alien forms, and we conform to the needs of a structure that is not based on human need, let alone an individual's."

Maia's breath sounded like snow. "But when we begin to live from within outward, in touch with the power of the erotic within ourselves, and allowing that power to inform and illuminate our actions upon the world around us, then we begin to be responsible to ourselves in the deepest sense. For as we begin to recognize our deepest feelings, we begin to give up, of necessity, being satisfied with suffering, and self-negation, and with the numbness which so often seems like the only alternative in our society. Our acts against oppression become integral with self, motivated and empowered from within."

Maia turned in her sleep and yawned. She seemed more a child now than a baby.

I kept reading from the Audre Lorde: "In touch with the erotic, I become less willing to accept powerlessness, or those other supplied states of being which are not native to me, such as resignation, despair, self-effacement, depression, self-denial."

I become less willing to accept powerlessness.
I become less willing to accept powerlessness.
I become less willing to accept powerlessness.

Poets and In-betweens

Lance tumbled in, singing. "I know it's only thirty-seven bucks and I promised a hundred, *buuut* . . . I found someone to help you with the baby."

Maia squealed and danced at the sight of him, hoping he'd put on a Clash album. There was no denying it: Lance was more fun than I was. He picked Maia up and swung her around.

"Watch!" she squealed. It was her new favorite word.

The caregiving company Lance worked for had assigned him a client who lived in the subsidized housing complex down the street, he said. He lit a cigarette, handed me the rest of the pack. "I asked the old lady what she's sick with, but she just said, 'I'm always dying and always keeping on.'"

I liked her already.

"If you could help her with the things they pay me to do," Lance said, "that'd save me time, and she could help you with the baby."

It sounded like a raw deal, the part about him collecting the money while his client and I worked, but the next day I knocked on Mary's door anyway, Maia perched on my hip.

Mary smiled at us. She was seventy, maybe, with

dyed black hair and laugh lines around her eyes. She wore beaded earrings and big, round glasses.

At her Formica kitchen table, she sang folk songs to Maia.

"Watch!" Maia laughed.

I washed Mary's dishes and put away her groceries and she kept singing while I wrote my microeconomic theory paper on her couch.

"You should come to my place for Christmas dinner," I said to Mary. I thought that being new in town she might not have anyplace else to go, and the woman from the food bank had called and promised me a turkey.

"Watch." Maia smiled.

"I'd be honored," Mary said, and she tussled Maia's hair and winked at her.

But a few weeks later when I went to pick up the turkey, it turned out to be two chickens—they'd run out of turkeys—and the woman at the food bank shrieked and backed away when she noticed I wasn't wearing any shoes.

Christmas: *Well, shit.*

We took the two chickens and a bag of potatoes.

"More?" Maia asked.

"We'll be fine with this, baby."

It had rained hard and we collected tree branches and brought them home and assembled them into an excellent Christmas tree–like structure, and Maia hung pieces of tinsel and yarn as decorations and she chanted, "Watch, watch," and I watched.

I had some carrots and some celery in the fridge. I

had some onions and I had a copy of *The Joy of Cooking*, so I made chicken potato stew for Christmas dinner.

"Don't skim off the fat," Mary said when I called to warn her about it not being a turkey after all. So it was greasy chicken stew for me and Mary and the baby.

We sat at my table in the alcove in our apartment, and Maia said, "Watch, watch," and we watched as she pretended to turn her stew into a turkey, and Maia listened intently as Mary told us this and that about her life. "See, I'm an in-between," Mary said. "Athabascan Indian and Scotch Irish." She was born on the Yukon River in Nulato, Alaska, in 1918, she said, but her mother died of tuberculosis and the white doctor who pronounced her dead adopted Mary into his family and took her to Seattle and away from everything she'd ever known.

I tried to picture Maia being taken away like that by a man who didn't look like her to a place where everything smelled different, but I didn't like the image and I shook it out of my mind.

Mary had been a legal secretary in Reno, she said, and didn't go back to Nulato until she was forty-six years old. "That's when I became a poet," she said. "When I went home. That's when I started writing poetry."

She'd lived in the Tenderloin in San Francisco for years, moved here to Petaluma because it's where they'd given her the government apartment. "Subsidized rent," she laughed, but she said her home was in Nulato and in the Tenderloin.

She gave me a book of her poems, *A Quick Brush of Wings*, and said, "Who are your ancestors, Ariel?"

I turned the book over in my hands, impressed. "Euro-mutts," I said. "A lot of them did things I'm not proud of. The other ones died in mental institutions."

Mary laughed at that. "If they weren't burned at the stake first!" She said, "Well, anyone who's evolving is an in-between. Sometimes you have to leave your people if you're going to evolve. Poets and in-betweens, we make our own families, and we don't worry too much about our differences."

"I want to be a writer," I admitted to Mary. "But nobody wants to publish my stories. So it's kind of unrequited, my want."

Mary shook her head the way she did. "Ariel, nobody has to publish your stories to make you a writer. We're writers talking right here. We're doing the things writers do every day. We're eating the chicken soup and soon we'll be washing the dishes and drinking tea. We're taking care of the children. We're paying attention, aren't we?"

"I guess."

"We're not guessing—we're helping each other," Mary said. She reached for her purse, frayed and brown, and she dug around in the pockets and produced a smooth, smoky-colored rock and she took my hand and she placed the rock in my palm and she said, "Moonstone. Hold it when you don't feel confident."

Maybe Mary was right. Maybe I didn't have to be the kind of writer who published stories and books, who they interviewed on the radio. Maybe I could be the kind of writer who helped other writers. I could be poor like Mary or not poor. I could be famous or not famous. I could belong to writing groups and play pool or I could be washing dishes and drinking tea. I could be always dying and always keeping on.

"Breathe in," Mary said, "and remember we always have plenty."

And I breathed in.

"Breathe out," she kind of chuckled, "and you'll feel better already."

"I have something else for you," Mary said when we dropped her off back at her apartment, and she rummaged through a cardboard file box on a side table. "Yes," she said. "This one. Take this one home with you." And she handed me a thick piece of paper with a poem letterpress printed on it.

See sister? How simple

even if we were
on the way to Astoria,
Bear Butte, Phoenix,
or Nulato,
we'd still be sitting
somewhere together drinking tea
and sister
if you ever stop
begging dreams from the sky
I will weep.
              —Mary TallMountain

At home, I set the moonstone on the built-in bookcase next to the garnet heart and the amber paperweight. I taped Mary's poem to the wall above and lit a candle.

Other people built altars to gods high in the sky. Maybe I would just build altars to the poets who lived in subsidized housing down the street. And,

See Mary? How simple

even if we were
on the way to San Francisco,
Oakland,
Portland,
Or the Petaluma food bank,
we'd still be sitting
here together at my cigarette-burned table
eating chicken stew I didn't skim the fat off of.

A Pretty Small Coven

The $547 monthly welfare check plus the $100 from my Gammie Evelyn was almost enough to pay the rent, but not quite. I needed to hustle the other $53, plus another $50 for the electricity bill, and $19 for the phone, and at least another $100 for diapers and conditioner and gas and stuff, so I did what I knew how to do: I stalked garage sales for underpriced used books.

Saturday mornings first thing, I'd get the newspaper and map our plan. Then we'd drive from sale to sale, and Maia would hunt for wooden train-track parts and hold them to her chest and say, "Mine," and I'd look for boxes of books marked twenty-five cents or fifty cents and I'd paw through, skipping the mass-market paperbacks and the Pritikin Diet guides, and I'd grab the cult classics and the hardbacks and the first editions and the small-press titles I knew I could get at least a couple of bucks for at the used bookstore on Fourth Street or at Copperfield's Underground on Kentucky. Another place in Santa Rosa was kind of hit or miss.

If we struck out at all three brick-and-mortar bookstores, last stop was a dealer in Cotati who wore a tie-dyed T-shirt and always had two VW vans full of books, and he'd at least give me back the fifty-cent investment and occasionally even slip me a Pat Califia or Susie Bright paperback with a little gleam in his eye as he said, "Get this out of here. I don't sell dirty books."

Of course that was a lie about him not selling dirty books. No paperback had better resale value than a Henry Miller. We both knew that. But I appreciated that he trusted me with the lesbian smut.

I didn't know where the guy who wore that tie-dyed T-shirt sold all those books he moved through those two vans. His operation was altogether bigger than mine. I imagined him cruising up and down the ocean cliffs of Highway One and stopping at all the little bookstores in all the little beach towns up and down the coast from British Columbia to Baja, and that's probably what he did.

Me, I'd flip twenty or thirty titles over the weekend and high-five Maia, and we'd stop at Markey's Café on Western Avenue for coffee and cookies and the weekly newspaper with our *Real Astrology* horoscopes—that was good enough to call success.

I read to Maia from her Aquarian oracle: "Do you recall the opening scene of Lewis Carroll's story *Alice's Adventures in Wonderland*? Alice is sitting outside on a hot day, feeling bored, when a white rabbit scurries by. He's wearing a coat and consulting a watch as he talks to himself. She follows him, even when he jumps into a hole in the ground. Her descent takes a long time. On the way down, she passes cupboards and bookshelves and other odd sights. Not once does she feel fear. Instead, she makes careful observations and thinks reasonably about her unexpected trip. Finally, she lands safely. As you do your personal equivalent of falling down the rabbit hole, Aquarius, be as poised and calm as Alice. Think of it as an adventure, not a crisis, and an adventure it will be."

Maia nodded solemnly.

"It's an adventure," I said again in that kind of baby talk that edges into desperation. "Not a crisis."

And Maia smiled a little at that. "Mine a-venta."

At home, she added the wooden train-track segments she'd found at the garage sales to her ever-expanding rail system, and she choo-chooed her wooden trains or colored blocks down those tracks and that was good enough to call happiness.

Afternoons, I smoked at the table and wrote stories about straight people without children who couldn't quite pinpoint the source of their existential depression.

It wasn't that I didn't *want* to write what I knew, but it seemed like only starving writers wrote about being starving writers, and I needed money so I had to figure out how to write about rich people. Even when I forced myself to try to write what I knew—*Write about a young mom, Ariel*—I'd just compulsively plagiarize Tillie Olsen and write, *I stand here ironing, and what you asked me moves tormented back and forth with the iron.* I mean, I'd never ironed, but that was pretty much the best first line I'd ever read, so where was I going to take mother literature from there, anyway? The world already had Tillie Olsen and Maya Angelou

and Adrienne Rich and Audre Lorde and Sharon Olds
and all the others. Those women probably had a coven.
And how could *I* get in? I couldn't even write that well
and they probably wouldn't think I was old enough,
anyway. Mary and the baby and I made for a pretty
small coven, but we were making do.

"We're making do," I whispered to Maia.

To Keep the Money Flowing

Every new moon, gather up as many bills and coins as you can find and place them on a windowsill that gets some moonlight. Don't count the money—you don't want to limit anything—just say your prayer to the moon, "Radiate wealth into my life with your sweet light."

In the morning, you can gather up the money and put it back in your wallet, but don't forget to say thank you and give the sky a little wink.

Womyn Helping Womyn

I found the blue flyer at Markey's Café in Petaluma:

Womyn Helping Womyn
Free baby clothes.
Free toys.
Utility bill vouchers.

I showed the flyer to the girl who sat next to me in economics. She was named after a tree—Birch, I think, or Ponderosa.

"I don't know why they spelled it like that," I told the tree-girl. "W-o-m-y-n."

Birch—or Ponderosa—sucked in her cheeks. She said, "Um, sister, they spelled it like that because we're trying to get the 'men' out of 'women.' It's called decolonization."

She raised her arched eyebrows, then reached back to collect her long hair in her fist and knot it into a bun.

I stared at her.

I'd been a girl for twenty-one years and I still didn't understand how other girls were so blasé in their perfect femme sexuality.

"I mean," the girl said, "do you just think of yourself as a woah-man? We're our own people, you know?

We're not just extensions of men. Can you believe that some womyn still call themselves *girls?*"

I studied the way the girl's stray locks of hair fell easily around her face. I wanted to tell her that I'd never thought of myself as a girl, but I knew I was too bad a liar.

I carried Maia in a red-checkered front pack even though she was almost too big for it, followed the directions on the flyer to the warehouse on the river where the womyn were helping womyn.

I got there a half hour early and sat down on a folding chair to nurse Maia. I covered us up, just a little, with a red baby blanket.

"*Mi'ja!*" the older woman scolded me as she came in carrying a giant box of baby toys. "You have to make it more obvious what you're doing."

I half smiled. "Excuse me?"

She had short, black hair, wore a flannel work shirt and brown construction boots. "For chrissake, if you're going to breastfeed, make it a public statement. Show some *teta*. We're expecting a hundred moms here today. Be an example."

I'd never thought much about breastfeeding as a statement—or an example. If we were out when Maia got hungry, I fed her. I mean, sure, I'd been asked to leave the yuppie cafés in San Francisco, but I was still shy and I didn't imagine I had any intrinsic right to be in anyone else's yuppie café. I felt embarrassed. I left.

Now I moved the baby blanket, showed the womyn some *teta*.

"There you go, *mi'ja*," she said. "Nobody's ever gonna

make a place for you in this world except you. Smash all the taboos. And when you're done feeding that baby get yourself a glass of water—stay hydrated—and come over here and help me get these vouchers organized. I'm short a volunteer."

"What do you do with your time?" the womyn asked as I approached her table, glass of water in hand. She took a pair of reading glasses out of her shirt pocket, put them on. "Besides pretending you're not breast-feeding and getting free clothes."

"I'm in college," I told her. "I'm studying economics, but I want to be a writer." I said that last part softly, so that maybe she wouldn't hear me, but she heard me.

She reached down and grabbed a slim newspaper from a milk crate on the floor under the table and held it out to me.

My hand shook as I took it from her. *Sonoma County Women's Voices*. I'd seen that paper at Markey's Café.

"It's the oldest continually published women's newspaper in the country. They always need editorial interns," she gave me a quick nod. "Now let's get these toys organized."

Utopia

The hippie girls in my women's studies class braided red and pink yarn into their long hair.

The punk girls didn't have any hair. They ran their fingers over their crew-cut scalps like they couldn't get enough of the texture.

All the girls said women were the gentler sex, the natural nurturers, yielding and receptive. All the girls spelled *womyn* with a *y*.

They said the vagina was "potential space" because its walls touched unless there was something in it—a penis, a dildo, a hand, a speculum, a baby, a government, a knife.

A book is potential space too. Its covers touch until you put a story in it.

I didn't talk much in that class. I didn't want to question the other girls' systems of meaning, so I just imagined myself as a tadpole in a jar. *Look, I've grown my little legs. I'm hop hop swim hop and away.*

Outside the classroom window, clouds formed themselves into frogs.

In *The Second Sex*, Simone de Beauvoir described the process of becoming a woman as an extended lesson in shame—a shame lived in the body.

The girls asked me to call them womyn. The womyn kept talking about womyn's natural empathy and non-violence. *Yes, I'm a little frog. I'm hop hop swim hop and away.*

When I was a kid, my mother always went for the skull. Fingernails across my scalp, she'd grab my hair like it was a handle and bash my head into the wall. *Cr-ack.*
I lived shame in my body.
I never saw my stepdad hit anyone. Sometimes he'd block my mother's punches with his open palm, but blocking is different from hitting.

Now the womyn had all read *Herland* and *The Dialectic of Sex* and they'd read *SCUM Manifesto* and they said we just had to figure out how to procreate without men.
"We should all major in science," one of the punk girls said, "and figure out how to manifest a perfect world without men."
"Womynifest," one of the hippie girls corrected her.
"We can genetically engineer all the babies to be girls," another girl offered.

All the womyn liked me. I'd practically procreated without a man so, *look*, children don't need fathers. Together we might all populate a perfect world of womyn separatists. The womyn liked me, too, because my baby was a girl and she wouldn't have to be exiled from our utopia when she turned eight or ten or twelve or fifteen or whatever age we decide that boy children become irreparably male.

I liked that the womyn liked me. Sometimes their inclusion felt fake, like they couldn't *not* like the single mom, but mostly I liked that they liked me. Yes, I liked that they liked me, but I still kept my hands up near my skull for quick blocking.

The Secret Lives of Witches

For *Sonoma County Women's Voices*, I covered Native American land rights. Back in 1971, a group of activists reclaimed 125 acres in Forestville and called it Ya-Ka-Ama. Now it was a thriving organic farm and the government wanted it back.

"Story of our lives," one of the original liberators of the land told me. "Story of our ancestors' lives."

I wanted to be the kind of writer who illuminated hidden injustice so starkly that it would simply cease to be perpetrated. *If only people knew that the government was retaking Native land! Everyone would be outraged!* It hadn't yet occurred to me that most people might feel fine about consciously exploiting other people.

For *Sonoma County Women's Voices*, I profiled poets. Mary TallMountain agreed to an interview about always dying and always keeping on.

"You'll have to be a warrior," she said. "Protect children and elders."

For *Sonoma County Women's Voices*, I wrote an article on domestic violence. The woman at the shelter gave me a xeroxed diagram showing the cycle of violence, and I ran my finger around the circle from the "build-up phase" to the "stand-over phase" to the "EXPLO-SION" to the "remorse phase" to the "pursuit phase" to the "honeymoon phase" and back to the "build-up phase." The violence of life had always seemed chaotic to me. This order mesmerized me. If violence could be charted and predicted with more accuracy than my period, surely it could be interrupted.

I kept running the pad of my index finger around the circle. My mother and Lance made more sense in this context. Even the man across the street and the angry men on the AM radio seemed to follow the same trajectory: Their rage bubbled up out of their own sense of impotence and they started to puff themselves up. They exploded and lashed out, but then they pulled back. They acted sorry but also minimized what had just happened, like, *Don't get hysterical, I don't even hit girls*, like, *It wasn't that bad. Geez, why so sensitive?* Then came the charming pursuit, the honeymoon or normalization that always fooled me and got me thinking, well, maybe they didn't mean all those things they said before when they started puffing themselves up— they're under a lot of pressure—and maybe that explosion wasn't so bad as it seemed. Yes, maybe it's just me, overreacting.

For *Sonoma County Women's Voices*, I wore a T-shirt that said "Nobody Knows I'm a Lesbian," and Maia and I rode in a bus full of activists into San Francisco to the march for women's lives, and it was just like the eighties when I was in high school and we demanded "US Out of Central America" but now it was "US Out of

My Uterus" and we marched and we chanted, "Think outside my box."

I wanted to be a superhero leftist journalist, like the love child of Lois Lane and Superman, but with Audre Lorde's intellect. We just had to let everyone know that shame wasn't helpful and white supremacy and racism could be overcome and women could decide for ourselves what to do with our bodies. Surely if we just got word out that god was pro-choice and pro–working class and pro–indigenous land rights, even the people in power would instinctively and humanely back down. Poor white people and poor people of color had so much in common—it was the wealthy dividing us with racism to keep us poor.

For *Sonoma County Women's Voices*, my editor called and asked if I could interview a local witch.

"Sure," I said. "I think I've heard of her."

My editor laughed. "Everyone's heard of her, Ariel."

So I packed Maia up with her Speak & Spell and dropped her off at Mary TallMountain's and drove the twenty miles north on Stony Point Road, past the boxy country houses and the mossy single-wide trailers, and I pulled up in front of a little brown house at the appointed hour. I climbed maybe twenty wooden steps and knocked on the south-facing red door. The row of shoes next to a frog statue on the porch cued me to take my boots off. "Oh, hey," I said as the witch opened the door. "Ariel Gore. *Sonoma County Women's Voices*."

The witch had a gap between her front teeth, wore her dark hair in two braids. I glanced down at her bare feet, admired her silver pedicure. When she held out her hand to shake mine, I felt self-conscious, like it mattered if she approved of the firmness of my grip. "Come in," she said.

Her living room smelled of burned sage and fresh lavender, looked like any bohemian living room with its potted plants hanging from hooks and set on top of bookshelves, too many books for all the bookshelves, too much art for the red-painted walls. An upright piano sat piled with more plants and books and art. *This is what grown-ups have*, I thought. *Plants and books and art*. I wanted to be a grown-up someday.

A wooden chest on the Persian rug in the middle of the living room served as a tea table, and the witch sat down on the carpet in front of it and motioned for me to sit on the other side. I stared at the large rose-quartz centerpiece.

"You're in charge of this interview, of course," the witch said as she poured jasmine tea into our cups and placed the black ceramic pot back on the table. "But what I had in mind was a glimpse into the life of a modern-day witch. People think we're extinct, that we were all burned at the stake. If they don't think we're extinct, they imagine we're either doing destructive magic or we're spaced out and stoned or we're conjuring Satan who, by the way, we don't believe in so would never conjure. Satan is a Christian invention." She shook her head. "I'd like to demystify the profession." She pushed a xeroxed, stapled booklet across the table. The cover pictured a compass rose under the title *Experimental Magick: The Secret Lives of Witches*.

"I have formal training in several schools of magic," the witch said, "but I believe we can pick and choose and experiment with what works. As long as we don't unleash anything that we wouldn't want unleashed on ourselves or our own children. We can use tried-and-true methods for expanding our consciousness and eventually casting spells, but we can also create our own meditations and write our own spells."

A cat jumped down from the top of the piano and purred as she rubbed herself against the witch.

I took out my notebook, wrote, *Glimpse into the life of a modern-day witch. We can write our own spells.* I sipped the tea.

"If you'll just excuse me for a moment," she said and stood up fast, and I watched as she walked through the kitchen and I listened as she opened and closed a back door.

I waited.

I drew daisies in my notebook.

I paged through the booklet, read: *Magick is a way of cultivating personal power and remembering our inherent divinity.*

I checked my cracked Swatch watch.

I stood up, called toward the kitchen, "Hello?"

All quiet.

I crept past the stove, looked out the witch's back window. It wasn't so much a yard out there as a whole redwood forest. I opened the door and let the cool air remind me not to be afraid. "Hello?"

The trees swallowed my voice and answered with the smell of damp bark.

I had a little pouch of tobacco in my pocket, so I sat down on the back step between the house and the forest and rolled myself a cigarette.

Where, oh where, has my famous witch gone?

The sun disappeared behind a charcoal cloud.

Dark, then bright.

The temperature shifts.

The smell of earth and moss.

I light my cigarette and savor the heat against my lungs as I inhale.

At first the trees stay quiet, like a place holding its breath. Then a rustling through the ferns. I scan the forest. That's when I see her—just behind a thin-trunked sequoia—a deer. We lock eyes for a moment. She stands perfectly still. I crush my cigarette, wipe the ashes onto my jeans, and stand up.

The deer turns and takes a few steps, then looks back at me like an invitation. I focus on her face between the evergreens and rhododendrons. She turns away and walks precariously along the edge of an open cleft in the earth. I follow her, redwood cones crackling under my bare feet on the cold ground. The deer keeps glancing back, then stops in front of a massive tree, looks back at me again as she steps into the hollow of the trunk.

I scramble, not wanting to lose her but not wanting to spook her either. I step into the tree and follow a staircase of roots that lead down into the earth.

At the bottom of the staircase, in the odd golden light

of a cave, I catch a glimpse of the deer again. "Where are we?" I whisper.

But the deer doesn't answer me.

The room glows, but I can't determine a light source. I study the deer's face, her alert ears, her dark nose circled by white fur. "Why did you bring me here?" I ask, then feel shy. *She* has *brought me here, hasn't she?*

The deer doesn't say anything. She sits down on a chair made of branches, sits as if she were more human now than hoofed animal. She folds her upper legs across her chest as if they're arms. I look into her broad-set eyes and for a flash of a moment I see the witch's eyes staring back at me. I take a sharp inhale, feel my chest tense. I want to ask so many things right then, but I just blink, and now her eyes are the eyes of a deer again.

I say, "Who are you?"

But the deer stays quiet.

I look around the strange cave-like room, walls made of dirt and rocks and ripped roots. *Maybe if I hold my breath, I can make this moment last longer.* And just then the deer nods very slowly and begins to speak to me in a voice so soft that I wonder if I'm imagining it: "I hope you don't mind meeting in our realm this time."

"Not at all," I whisper, shaky.

She says, "This is the next stage of your initiation that you yourself began even before you were cut."

I stare at her. I want to pretend that I don't know what she's talking about, but I nod.

"We realize that was traumatic," she says.

I feel disoriented. My scar aches.

The deer says, "As you may have already gathered,

your particular assignment is to tend to the degraded feminine, the shamed feminine." The deer wiggles her shoulders in a gesture different from a shrug. The root walls around her glow more golden. "There are a number of you with the same assignment. You'll work mostly alone, but you'll meet the others over time." The deer pauses, twitches her ears. "We are aware that you'll require complete freedom to write about your personal experiences, but we ask that you be discreet when it comes to disclosing anything beyond the most superficial details about the realm itself or the others you meet here."

I keep nodding. My lips feel dry.

From her chair of branches, the deer stares at me. She says, "What does shame require to stay alive? What is the antidote to shame?" And without waiting for me to answer, she stands up on her four legs and turns and walks away from me farther into the earth, this time not looking back.

I stand there in the strange cave for a long time, just breathing. Finally, I turn around to make my way back up the stairway of roots, toward the hollow of the tree trunk, and back out into the bright afternoon.

The contrast between the cool air and the pale light of the sun makes me feel alive in a way I can't remember having felt in a long time, but I'm not quite sure what's happened.

I open the back door to the witch's kitchen. "Hello?"

The witch calls back to me. "Is that you, Ariel?" She sits on her Persian rug sipping her tea as if I'm the one who left her there waiting and not the other way around.

The lights flickered off for a moment.

Then bright.

I checked my watch. "I actually have to go. I have to pick up my daughter from her babysitter." I'd promised Mary I wouldn't be long.

The witch smiled a nostalgic smile. She said, "I had a baby when I was a teenager too. But I'm a little older than you are, and they sent me to a home in San Francisco and told me I had to sign away my son to a married couple I couldn't meet and I was never to speak of the experience—or of my child—again."

I stood quiet. So often, with people, I just didn't know what to say.

The witch said, "Don't worry. You don't have to say anything. It's just a herstory you should know."

I kept silent, but I felt like such a dick right then, not saying anything. I felt a new kind of shame, too, this time at my extreme privilege of having been allowed to keep my child.

I wanted to say *I'm so sorry that happened to you.*

I wanted to say *I'm having the hardest time.*

I wanted to say *I don't know how to be a woman.*

I wanted to say *I'm afraid.*

But I just nodded again and said, "Thank you," and my hands shook because I was afraid of people who were older than me but not old enough to be my grandmother.

The witch walked me to the door, said, "If you don't like the fairy tales you've been handed, Ariel, you don't have to conform to them. You can reauthor them. You can write your story however you choose."

As I headed home, past the run-down trailers and the old white farmhouses, I thought of what my mother's friend Roberta had said, too, about being sent to homes where their babies were stolen, and I wondered how many of the women I passed on the street every day held the same secret. I wondered, too, how I could write the witch's profile for *Sonoma County Women's Voices*. Maybe we'd have to make a new date for the interview.

I picked Maia up from Mary TallMountain's, and that's when I noticed that Mary had a frog statue next to the red front door of her place too.

Grown-up witches have frog statues.

On the way back to our apartment, I stopped at the Zen nursery, bought a small rose-quartz crystal, and put a stone frog statue on layaway.

That night for dinner, Maia and I ate cheese-and-tomato sandwiches by candlelight. "Hot," I warned Maia as I pointed to the flame.

"Ooooh," she cooed, rocking back and forth in the shadow of the candlelight. "Haaaa."

She was adaptable, my baby.

I pressed a button to check my answering machine, and here was my editor from *Sonoma County Women's Voices* saying she'd heard that the famous witch canceled on me at the last minute and sorry about that, don't worry, we'll have another assignment for you soon.

When a Woman Thinks Alone

Insatiable
Ariel Gore
Women's Lit 104

> "All witchcraft comes from carnal lust,
> which in women is insatiable."
>
> —*The Malleus Maleficarum*, the go-to European
> witch-hunting manual first published in 1487

The greatest risk factor for being accused, tried, convicted, and executed for witchcraft in fifteenth- to seventeenth-century Europe was to have a female body.

The second greatest risk factor was poverty.

Add to those risk factors having a job or being sexual or single or outspoken or an unwed mother or unconcerned with cultural beauty norms or mentally ill or a healer—especially a midwife or a counselor—and you were pretty much dead. Dare to help another woman find contraceptives, and you were dead. Have the audacity to be old and grumpy, and you were most certainly dead.

"When a woman thinks alone," *The Malleus Maleficarum* warned, "she thinks evil."

At least one hundred thousand people were killed as witches. Some researchers put the number closer to a million. The vast majority of those killed were poor women. Men were murdered, too, and children and middle-class people, but the vast majority were poor women. And it wasn't a case of mass hysteria. The witch trials were a calculated campaign of terror financed and carried out by the ruling class against working-class and difficult women to establish the supremacy of Christian, white patriarchy and Western medicine for profit.

It may be important to note that public torture and executions weren't reserved solely for those accused of witchcraft. As the French philosopher Michel Foucault points out in *Discipline and Punish: The Birth of the Prison*, public humiliation, torture, and murder were, at least through the 1700s, the standard way for European sovereigns to inscribe their power onto the bodies of rebels and criminals. Later, governments would find less violent, more insidious ways to control our bodies.

The crimes women were accused of—and often confessed to under torture—ran the rainbow from causing droughts to attending hard births to having sex with the devil.

When damaging hailstorms hammered Wiesensteig, Germany, sixty-seven women were blamed for the weather and burned alive.

In 1629 alone, nine hundred witches were killed around Würzburg.

In the Trier area, two villages were left with just one female inhabitant each.

The murdered women couldn't leave us their stories.

What feminist historians know comes to us from the court records kept by the persecutors and from the hundreds of witnesses to each witch's public torture and execution.

We know, for example, that Walpurga Hausmännin was a licensed midwife and elderly. We know that after she was widowed at a relatively young age, she had at least one lover. Her story comes to us in her own words under torture, from the judge's promptings, and from a court-reporter's opinion. Walpurga apparently confessed to all that she'd been charged with: the deaths of more than forty babies, two women in childbirth, eight cows, and a horse. Her neighbors accused her of bringing on a hailstorm and causing three adults to languish until they, too, died.

The people in Walpurga's village had relied on her for healing, but now they scapegoated her for all their tragedies. She shared a meal with a woman named Magdalena, then Magdalena blamed her for her premature labor. She gave a little boy a hobbyhorse to ride, and when he later died, people said she'd given it to him so that he'd "ride on it till he lost his sense." She once helped a man push a cart. Eight years later as he died, all fingers pointed to Walpurga. She gave a young girl a drink and, years later, when the girl got sick, Walpurga was suspect. Every minor kindness was reframed as a crime.

She was female.

She was poor.

She'd had a lover outside of marriage.

She was a woman thinking alone.

She was a midwife.

In 1587 she was sentenced to death.

For her service and her sexuality, men stripped Walpurga naked, tied her to a cart, and marched her through the streets of her hometown, stopping several times before they reached the execution place. At the first stop, outside the town hall, they cut off her left breast and tore her right arm with red-hot iron rods. At the second stop, they cut off her right breast. At the third stop, outside the gates of the hospital, they tore her left arm. At the fourth stop, her left hand. At the place of her execution, men first cut off her right hand—the hand with which she'd made her oath as a midwife—and in front of the gathered crowd, they burned her alive.

A butterfly fluttered off.

The town Walpurga had served her whole life didn't even want her ashes—men scooped them up and dumped them in a stream.

Witches turn into butterflies when they die.

My phone rang in the dark. My Gammie Gore. She drank gin instead of vodka. She said, "Is that you, Ariel?" As if someone else might answer my phone. She said, "Honey? What are you doing?"

I rolled a cigarette, told my Gammie Gore about my final paper for the semester, about all the women who were burned or hanged or drowned.

My Gammie Gore didn't say anything.

I could hear the ice cubes clink, gently, in her tumbler. I opened the window to let in the night air, blew the smoke from my cigarette outside. "In some villages in Trier, Germany, just one female inhabitant survived."

"Trier?" my Gammie Gore chirped, almost cheerful. "That's where my grandfather Otto came from."

"Your grandfather?" I exhaled. And right then it occurred to me that my body existed now only because my DNA hid inside a white man's.

Best
Disguise
Ever.

I wondered how my ancestors felt as they watched their town midwife—the one who had delivered them and all their siblings and all their children safely into this world—as she was cut and tortured.

I wondered how the witnessing changed them.

I wondered how it changed their fears for their daughters and for their granddaughters.

How it changed their reaction to being handed a girl-baby.

"Honey?" my Gammie Gore piped up.

"Yes, Gammie?" *How long had I been silent?*

"Honey, I was actually calling to tell you that Grandpa and I are getting a new television."

I took a drag from my cigarette and blew smoke rings like I used to in high school, gently crushed the burning cherry into my wrist. "That's great, Gammie."

"Honey, I was actually calling to tell you that Grandpa and I want you to have our *old* television."

I nodded into the phone like my Gammie Gore could

see me. "Really?" When I was a kid, my grandparents' fat television symbolized wealth to me. I said, "Thanks for thinking of us, Gammie." And I meant it. *That fat television.*

The witch hunts in Europe coincided with the rise of Western medicine as a profit-based and exclusively male profession. The witch hunts coincided, too, with the expansion of European imperialism and the European slave trade in Africa. The more territory European colonists claimed, the more people they enslaved overseas, the more women they publicly murdered at home.

Ironically, this whole era in European history is known as "The Renaissance."

The last witch was burned to death in Europe in 1782, but not because misogyny ended. Foucault notes in *Discipline and Punish*, "It was a time when, in Europe and in the United States, the entire economy of punishment was redistributed." New, modern codes were planned and drawn up. While execution would remain in the arsenal of punishment, torture as a public spectacle virtually disappeared. The new torture would cut and burn the soul. The new public spectacle would hold us up as objects of shame. Foucault writes: "From being an art of unbearable sensations, punishment has become an economy of suspended rights."

If we don't follow society's rules, we risk losing our freedom. But if we must follow those rules without question, we've already given up our freedom.

*

I turned in my final paper, but this time my hand didn't shake so much. I guessed that my women's lit professor who looked like Susan Sontag, only hotter, would suggest I take out the part about my Gammie Gore, but I didn't care.

I hadn't slept in a long time.

Street signs looked blurry on the road.

I thought about silence and the way people can intimidate each other so deeply; it lasts for generations, for centuries.

I thought about shame, and the way my Gammie Gore called me irresponsible and the way I couldn't tell her that that's why we weren't friends anymore. It wasn't that I didn't love her. It was just all the shame, my body paraded naked.

I wanted to call her back and say, *Gammie? Do you understand what it means that your grandfather Otto was from Trier? Do you understand everything we've had to hide? Do you understand that it's not our cut bodies and our schizophrenia and our teenage sexuality that we should be ashamed of? When did we become them and turn on ourselves?*

But I didn't pick up the phone.

I left it, silent, on the table.

I thought about butterflies.

Toshiba

Delivery men in blue shorts brought my
  grandparents' television.

The television brought the Gulf War.

Brought *Sesame Street.*

Brought Anita Hill testifying against
  Clarence Thomas.

Brought *Northern Exposure.*

Brought Rodney King the night he was
  beaten by the LAPD.

Brought *Beverly Hills, 90210.*

Brought the Los Angeles uprising.

Brought *Murphy Brown.*

Brought Dan Quayle.

Brought "family values."

A Beautiful Day in This Neighborhood

Three Explanations for the End of Our Suburban Experiment:

1. The alternative college outside Petaluma, California, filed for bankruptcy and would close at the end of my sophomore year.

    This is true.

    It's the explanation I gave most people who asked.

2. When my Gammie Gore gifted us her old color television and I set it up on top of a milk crate in the living room and I sat down on the blood-stained carpet and I *click-clicked* through the channels to PBS and a documentary about the Mills College strike in Oakland, California, girls I was pretty sure called themselves womyn cried and chanted on a green campus because the school's board had voted to go coed and these womyn didn't want men at their school.

    I watched them cry and chant.

    They were lesbians, I was pretty sure. I'd never seen lesbians on television before. Except, you know, tennis players. The lesbians crying on television mesmerized me as they chanted their demands. At the end of the documentary, when the board reversed its decision to go coed, the womyn cried tears of victory and they made a letterpress broadside that said,

We had a revolution.
There was childcare.
There was consensus.
We sent thank-you notes.
We cleaned up after ourselves.
And we won.
We won!

There were lesbians in Oakland.
And childcare.
This is true.
It's the explanation I gave myself.

3. I can still feel the weight of Maia's toddler body on my hip as I climbed the few steps to our apartment door. I can feel her little hand resting on my bicep. I can hear her babbling the words she didn't yet have. And my breath still catches in my rib cage when I see it—even only in the mind's eye of my memory: A plastic baby doll spray-painted red and crucified to our front door with two knives. In black sharpie on the wood of the door behind the bloodied doll, someone had written: *Die welfare slut.*

This is true too.
It's the real reason we left.

It's the only reason for the end of our suburban experiment.

I covered Maia's eyes with my free hand, glanced toward the nice beige house on the other side of the cul-de-sac, but I didn't see anyone.

I swallowed hard, like some instinctive attempt to make the tyranny my own.

I pushed the door open fast so that Maia wouldn't see the horror-movie doll. I sat her down in front of the new television. I turned on Mr. Rogers and I blinked at him in his cardigan sweater as he assured us that it was *a beautiful day in this neighborhood and a neighborly day in this beauty wood. Would you be mine? Could you be mine?*

I packed our things fast. I wondered if I was focusing on the wrong details, but it seemed odd to me that the baby doll wasn't even ours. It wasn't something Maia had left on the lawn. I mean, had someone gone out and bought a plastic baby doll specifically intending to spray-paint it red and crucify it to our door with *die welfare slut*? Or did they have kids of their own and they'd stolen this doll from their kid? I wondered if focusing on the wrong details was an early symptom of hysteria. How long before I ended up committed to a warehouse asylum for indigents?

My *Real Astrology* horoscope advised me to consciously reverse the meaning and flip the context of my most traumatic imprints, but what did that mean?

Right then my most traumatic imprints seemed to be the image/memory of my mother smashing my head into the wall when I was a kid, having my vagina cut when I was tied down to the metal table at nineteen and expecting the goddess, and now the spray-painted baby doll crucified to my apartment door in this town I'd never quite taken to.

I remembered the deer underground in the witch's backyard and the cave with root walls and I thought, *What if none of my imprints mean what I think they mean?*

Maybe I could rewrite the fairy tale of my life, transforming every blow to the head, and every cut to the cunt, and every crucified doll into some kind of an initiation.

Maybe this could be my new genre: the memoirist's novel. My words could form a magical spell, like an alchemical furnace, built with the conscious intention of transmuting shame into power.

Oakland.

The East Bay.

Yes, we would move to Oakland, and I would go to school with the crying lesbians and we would build altars to Artemis and to Walpurga Hausmännin and to Rapunzel and to Augustine Gleizes and to Tillie Olsen and to Mary TallMountain and to Maya Angelou and to Adrienne Rich and to Audre Lorde and to Luisah Teish and to my Gammie Evelyn, who I still loved like a tomato.

The Mills College admissions office hadn't called me back yet, so my arrival remained in the realm of potential, but if I'd learned anything in my twenty-one years it was how to leave a place.

I am the malignity, after all.

But I am also the escape.

I sorted our things into garbage bags to throw away and garbage bags to pack into the car. I called my landlord, left a message telling him that I had to go, then packed up the phone and the TV too. I carried out the three keeper bags and pressed one into the back seat and two into the hatchback. As I picked up the stone frog statue from next to our front door and carried the weight of it to the car, I felt a moment of nostalgia for a dream I'd never quite allowed to bloom in me—the one where a young mother and child can live unbothered in a small American town—but as I buckled the frog into the front passenger's seat with Maia's witch doll, the frog sighed and whispered in my ear, *We don't get to root. This is a move-along world.*

"Go, Mama?" Maia asked, all cheeks.

I buckled her into her car seat. "Go, Maia," I said. I walked around the car and climbed into the driver's side, didn't buckle my own seat belt, started the ignition, and we rolled out of that cul-de-sac—me and the frog and the witch doll and the baby easing out of suburbia for good or for bad.

I turned right on Petaluma Boulevard and headed for the highway, Sinéad O'Connor on the cassette player singing about how if they hated her they would hate me. We drove fast past fields, past cows and their shit, past the boxy white farmhouses. I didn't know what a plastic doll spray-painted red and crucified to our front door meant to the person who'd left it there, but to me it meant I would never have a fireplace. I tried to shrug it off, like, *People around here are really fucking psychotic*, but I held it in my breath too. I guess some part of me believed it—that I needed to *die welfare slut.* And I grieved my own self-hatred. Would some part of me always believe the bullies who hated me? *I didn't deserve to have a child. I could only do a terrible job as a mother and she would always suffer for it. Maybe they were right that the only hope for me was to find some man to marry me and leave my ideas of independent artist/mother behind me.*

Where could we go?

1. My mother and stepfather's house, where Roberta hissed at me and turned herself into a possum.
2. My Gammie Gore's house on Carmel Beach, where I'd see *irresponsible* written on every wall.
3. My Gammie Evelyn's house in Orange County, where we'd start drinking at breakfast.

I pictured sitting down with Maia at each of the three dining-room tables, and I could already taste the sour shame sandwiches.

What would I tell them, anyway, about why we'd left Petaluma?

I didn't know anyone in Oakland, but I did know someone in San Francisco. I pushed eject, and here was all the omen I needed: Sweet Honey in the Rock harmonizing on KPFA.

"Way go, Mama?" Maia singsonged from the back seat.

"We're going to Jamie's house in San Francisco," I announced like it had been my summer plan all along.

Maia laughed in the rearview. "Go Safacisco."

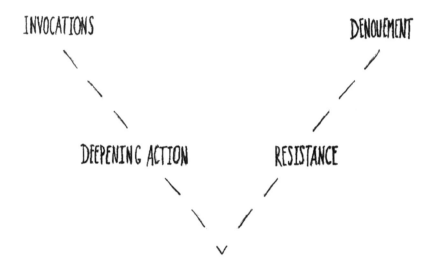

This is the stylistic center of my book.

If we invert Freytag's pyramid,
what belongs at the center of a book?

Perhaps not a culminating climax
so much as potential space.

BOOK 3
Resistance

A Closet with a Window in It

From *Experimental Magick:*
The Secret Lives of Witches:

When we talk about magick, we do not mean to
suggest that anything is easy. You cast your spell
like you cast a fishing line. Fishing is work. Fish-
ing is invocation. Fishing is calling the fish to us.
Not every line cast will reel something in.

Magick isn't the absence of obstacles or hard
work or even wrong-direction hopes. Magick is
the steady development of personal power in the
pursuit of a world beyond the white-supremacist,
capitalist war machine that depends on misogyny
as its helix foundation.

*

The portal to Jamie's Mission-district apartment was
just a dirty white metal door staring blankly out from
between a taqueria and a botanica candle shop that
advertised no-fee check cashing.

I pressed the buzzer, then felt awkward standing
there with Maia on my hip as Jamie opened the door in
her baggy jeans and tight tank top. I tried to swallow

the embarrassed feeling, said, "Hey, um, so we just need a place to crash for maybe a month?" I bit my lip hard until I tasted blood. "I mean, a month *maximum*."

Jamie laughed, resigned to us, and I appreciated that, but her girlfriend glared at us from the top of the red carpeted stairs. The girlfriend looked kind of like me, with curly and disheveled hair, but she was maybe thirty pounds heavier and had a dramatic line of bruised and bloody needle holes that ran along the vein-line of her arm.

"It's just a walk-in closet," Jamie was saying as we followed her up the stairs and down a creaking hallway.

The girlfriend kept glaring at me. Her face was the face anyone would make if their lover's incredibly sexy ex showed up unannounced and all fertile with a baby on her hip and said, "A month *maximum*," and kind of pouted her lips when she said it, and that made me feel important in an unfamiliar and competitive kind of way. I knew it was wrong to bask in Jamie's girlfriend's jealousy, but I'd never been anything like *that woman* before and the small power of it suited me.

It also suited me that Jamie's walk-in closet had a little window in it.

A closet with a window in it, I decided right there, is a workable thing.

I dragged our garbage bags of clothes and toys and books up the stairs.

Maia carried her witch doll. She said, "Up, up, up."

I winked at her.

And she winked back the witchiest wink I'd ever seen a baby wink and I felt suddenly unsettled—like she wasn't just my doll. She was a girl-child separate from me. And she would someday become more powerful.

"Up, up, up," I whispered back.

That first afternoon arranging our things, I felt like a traveler and I wasn't sure I liked the feeling anymore. It had held me comfortably alone before the baby, but as a mother I wondered if a closet could really be enough.

Maia didn't seem to mind. And it was only temporary. *A month maximum*, I reminded myself, like the reminding would make it true.

What was I doing?

I wondered if the people from the AM radio shows could take Maia from me if they found us here. I wondered if the police could take her. Or Child Protective Services.

Is a closet with a window really a workable thing?

Should I have put her up for adoption like they say on the AM radio?

Am I die welfare slut?

Part of me regretted not bringing the crucified doll from Petaluma with us because now in my self-doubt I questioned whether it had existed at all. It seemed too weird and random—like some serious satanic shit—like that cul-de-sac in Petaluma had been more seventeenth century than 1992. I thought of how I felt when I first saw that young mom moving into the nice beige house on the other side of the cul-de-sac. *Hopeful*. Like I might make a friend. Like Maia might have a little neighborhood friend. Like I might break us out of our echoing isolation.

I mean,

I made that bitch muffins.

*

I left Maia in Jamie's closet playing with her Speak & Spell, and I stepped into Jamie's kitchen to make a mozzarella-and-tomato sandwich.

Jamie's girlfriend glared at me from the table, took a hit from her orange bong, said, "So, you're in the closet?" and she laughed like that was the funniest thing. "In the closet, get it?"

I wanted badly to like Jamie's girlfriend.

I wanted badly to hate Jamie's girlfriend.

Mostly I wanted to be back in my own little apartment in Petaluma with my own little muddy backyard and Jimmy Cliff on the cassette player and no changes. I sliced the cheese thick for our sandwiches. "Yep," I said. "I'm in the closet."

I crept into the closet with our sandwiches.

Maia sat on the floor, a black cat curled in her arms.

"Where did you get that cat, Maia?"

She gestured toward the window. It was maybe three inches open, but no ledges or fire escape led to it. "Luna," she smiled all witchy. She'd already named it.

*

At bedtime, Luna purred as I read to Maia from Gloria

Anzaldúa: "The struggle is inner: Chicano, *indio*, American Indian, *mojado*, *mexicano*, immigrant Latino, Anglo in power, working-class Anglo, Black, Asian—our psyches resemble the bordertowns and are populated by the same people. The struggle has always been inner, and is played out in outer terrains. Awareness of our situation must come before inner changes, which in turn come before changes in society. Nothing happens in the 'real' world unless it first happens in the images in our heads."

Was this closet the bordertown of my psyche?

I could hear Jamie and her girlfriend giggling romantic through the wall.

As Maia closed her eyes, I whispered to her from Gloria Anzaldúa, "I will not be shamed again. Nor will I shame myself."

I needed new images in my head.

After Maia fell asleep, I switched to reading *Susie Sexpert's Lesbian Sex World*. What I loved about all the feminist writers was that they made me feel that if something *happened*, that made it relevant. It didn't have to be a big deal or a small deal. It didn't have to be happening only to men or only to white people or only to straight people. If it *happened*, it mattered. Mama feminism didn't judge.

Susie Bright said, *Don't be ashamed of your sexual illiteracy, just remedy it.*

War or skinned knee or sexual illiteracy, mama feminism wanted to hear about it all. She wanted to dust us off, end our racism and our misogyny, bring us to orgasm, and send us on our way to succeed or fail with love.

I closed my eyes and prayed to all the goddesses I could think of: Let us grow strong. Let us grow bound up with amazement. Let us grow fat.

Nobody's Going to Save You

Monday afternoons in San Francisco, we picked up our weekly allotment of fresh carrots and lettuce and apples and tamales from the food pantry at the Women's Building on Eighteenth Street—no questions asked.

We bought cat food for Luna at the corner store. Jamie and her girlfriend claimed they'd never seen the cat before, didn't know where it could have come from.

We stopped at the weird anarchist shop on Valencia, across from New College, and picked up a xeroxed zine for punk parents called *The Future Generation*.

In Jamie's sunny kitchen, her girlfriend squinted at us as I sat Maia down and filled a steamer with tamales. "Are you hungry?" I asked the girlfriend.

The girlfriend's squint seemed friendlier than her glare. She shrugged, pushed a copy of *Sun, Moon, and Talia* by Giambattista Basile across the table, and that's when I noticed that the track marks on her arm were actually a tattoo of track marks, and I didn't know what to make of that. *Like, maybe she used to shoot up and she wanted to remember? Or maybe it was some San Francisco joke I didn't get?*

Jamie's girlfriend belonged to writing groups.

Jamie's girlfriend played pool.

And now Jamie's girlfriend had track marks tattooed down her arm.

She pointed to the book, said, "It's the original 1634 version of *Sleeping Beauty*." And she nodded toward Maia like surely Maia was a big Sleeping Beauty fan, but Maia just played with her food-pantry apple slices because she'd never heard of Sleeping Beauty. Not yet.

I opened the book.

Once upon a time, it began. That's how they always began. Like every story has its era—its moment, even—and the story couldn't or wouldn't exist in any other moment in history: I'm a queer unwed mother who was allowed to keep her baby and who is now holed up in a large, walk-in closet in a run-down apartment in the Mission in San Francisco when apartments in the Mission in San Francisco were maybe $850 a month. *Once upon a time.*

Once upon a time, a wealthy single dad sent for astrologers to predict his infant daughter's destiny, but when those seers calculated her horoscope, they saw the worst and warned the father that the girl ought to watch out for splinters from flax.

"Flax?" the father said. "We can get rid of the flax!" It didn't occur to him that "flax" might be symbolic of women's work because that's what everyone used to make linen and lace, so the man ordered all the flax—and all the hemp, while he was at it—out of the house.

Done.

Adulthood would never arrive.

(Some people hate women without consciously hating girls.)

The single dad's baby, Talia, grew up happy and

sheltered, but adolescence comes with or without flax, and now Talia wasn't that knobby-kneed kid playing by the creek's edge. She sighed, bored as she watched the street from her bedroom window. When she saw an old woman pass by spinning on a spindle, she called out to her, "What are you doing?"

The old woman stopped and told Talia about work and the way it was sometimes a drag and sometimes engaging and liberating.

Talia nodded and asked to stretch some flax.

The old woman didn't see any harm in showing Talia how to work, but as soon as Talia reached out to the spinster, a splinter of flax caught under her fingernail, and she fainted unconscious.

The old woman panicked. She knew what happened to old women who got caught talking to young women. What had she been thinking? There had been witch trials and executions all over Europe that year. The old woman cursed herself. How could she be so stupid? She rushed off and she didn't look back.

When Talia's father got home, his heartbreak morphed instantly into denial. *No, she could not be dead! He would not bury her!* Instead, he dressed her in her most beautiful clothes, took her out to one of his country estates, and placed her on a throne in one of the rooms.

Then he abandoned the property.

An abandoned estate can be a tower.

Time passed. One day a king hunted in the forest near the old estate, and his falcon escaped from him and flew into one of the windows of the palace, meaning that his entitlement—symbolized by the falcon—entered the building even before he did. The king knocked on the door, but there was no answer. The door was locked. So the king, following his entitlement, scaled the wall and climbed through a window.

Inside, the king wandered from room to room, supposedly looking for his falcon—looking for his entitlement, as classic home invasion—until at last he came to a large, beautiful drawing room, where he found the unconscious girl, raped her, and left her for dead.

It wasn't the first time Talia had been left for dead.

But she wasn't dead. And now, still in a coma, she was pregnant. When she went into labor, fairies who looked like butterflies attended her birth. They set Talia's twins—a boy and a girl—to nurse at her breasts. When one of the babies couldn't find Talia's nipple, she sucked at her mother's fingertip instead, drawing out the splinter of flax, and Talia awoke as an unwed mother and gave her children the total hippie names Sun and Moon, and she nursed them until they were fat and satisfied.

Back at the castle, the king remembered raping Talia as she lay unconscious, and the memory of it made him feel important. He wanted to do it again. He told his wife he was going hunting, but he journeyed to the estate instead, his entitlement swelling in his chest. He scaled the wall of the castle as he'd done before. He walked through the rooms like he owned them. But he froze when he found Talia and her kids awake and thriving. Now the king knew he had to do some fast talking, but the king was a fast talker and Talia had been asleep a long time, so, with all his narcissistic charm, he explained what had happened and how Talia had come to be a mother unconsciously. The pair hung out for a few days, drinking beer, and this time when the king left her alone it was with the promise that he'd come back for them soon, and he went off, feeling like a real suave savior.

At home, the king couldn't stop thinking about Talia and the kids. He called out their names in his sleep.

The queen mouthed their names to herself and her heart hurt, but by morning her heartbreak had morphed into pure jealousy. She went to her husband's secretary and demanded: "Tell me who his lover is or I'll have you killed."

The secretary told. Of course he told.

The queen nodded into the names, sent the secretary to Talia with a forged note from the king, saying, *Send the children—I miss them.*

Now, Talia was trusting. And Talia could certainly use the childcare. So Talia obeyed. She'd never listened to the AM radio that might have warned her about people and vengeance and the way they wanted to take our kids away and put them in orphanages.

So off the kids went. And the queen was hardcore. When Sun and Moon got there, she marched them into the kitchen and told her cook to roast them for dinner.

That night as they ate, the queen kept nudging her husband to eat more, saying, "You're eating what's your own."

The next day the queen sent the secretary back to

get Talia herself—and of course Talia was rested by now and thrilled at the chance to join her kids. Imagine her horror when she was brought instead to the queen who fumed, "Are you the welfare slut who has been enjoying my husband?"

Talia tried to reason with the queen, telling her that she hadn't enjoyed it—that the king had raped her as she slept and then come back all entitled like he was the children's rightful parent.

The queen didn't care. She commanded that a huge fire be lit in the palace courtyard and that Talia be burned at the stake like so many witches.

Talia, stalling for time, knelt before the queen and begged as a last request that she be allowed to do a proper striptease. It had been a long time since anyone had offered to strip for the queen and Talia's offer turned her on, but the show would be more rape culture than sensual. As Talia removed each garment, she screamed the terror of all her traumatic imprints, and tears streamed down her face as she viscerally remembered each one: Her father keeping her from school and work, her coma, her abandonment in the old palace, her captivity, her rape, the kidnap and possible murder of her children, and now the fire that burned, hungry for her female body.

Now, as the king returned from his man cave, he heard the screaming and found his mistress almost naked and his wife about to throw her in the fire. He demanded an explanation, and that's when the queen told him that he'd unknowingly eaten his own children—and that his rape victim was about to be burned for a whore.

He was appalled that he'd eaten his kids, and he commanded that the queen herself should be burned alive—along with his sell-out secretary. So it was that two more people were burned alive without trials.

The last to be executed would be the cook, but when they dragged him out, he cried, "Sire, I saved your children. They're not dead. I hid them with my wife." The cook then called his wife to bring Sun and Moon to the king, "who covered them with kisses and caresses; in fact, he could not get enough of kissing and embracing both the children and their mother, as he gathered them all into his arms."

They were all creeped out by the king's touches, but they stayed silent for survival's sake.

Talia married her rapist, and they became the model of nuclear families that would last for centuries.

*

"That's a psychotic story," I said to Jamie's girlfriend as I closed the book and pushed it back across the table.

She smirked. "Shall we call you Talia?"

I didn't know what she meant by that. *Like, did she want me to strip for her before she burned me alive?*

That night, I read to Maia from *Borderlands/La Frontera* by Gloria Anzaldúa: "Nobody's going to save you. No one's going to cut you down, cut the thorns thick around you. No one's going to storm the castle walls nor kiss awake your birth, climb down your hair, nor mount you onto the white steed. There is no one who will feed the yearning. Face it. You will have to do, do it yourself."

Maia yawned a round baby yawn and closed her eyes.

I woke disoriented in the still-dark night, a streetlight glowing through the window, and I blinked twice because here's a woman sitting next to me on our futon. I sit up slowly, surprised but not afraid. "Susie?" It's Susie Bright from *Susie Sexpert's Lesbian Sex World* right here next to me in the closet. *Like, what is happening?* She wears a floppy felt hat, arm warmers, and nerd glasses just like in her picture in the book. I say, "Susie Sexpert, is that you?"

And she smiles friendly, not coy like I'd picture a porn writer.

I say, "Susie, kiss me awake."

And she gives me a quick kiss.

My breasts press against my T-shirt, heavy with milk, and Susie says, "May I touch them?"

I take my shirt off, slow, like a striptease.

When she touches my breasts, the milk shoots out in perfect arcs toward her and she laughs, which makes me laugh.

Susie Sexpert doesn't rape me in my sleep like the king in *Sleeping Beauty*. She doesn't even really wake me up. She just whispers, "You will have to do it yourself," as she fades back into my dream.

And in the morning, my shirt clings to me, wet with milk.

The Feminist Agenda

"The feminist agenda is not about equal rights for women," Pat Robertson announced in 1992. "It's about a socialist, antifamily political movement that encourages women to leave their husbands, kill their children, practice witchcraft, destroy capitalism, and become lesbians."

I nodded at the televangelist's revelations. I'd never wanted to kill my child, but the rest of what he said rang true. The rest of it rang very true to me.

Goals and reminders for 1992:
Don't get married, ever.
Practice witchcraft.
Destroy capitalism.
Get into the lesbian college.

Reject

All of San Francisco glowed blue and flickered like a hallucination.

My landlord in Petaluma forwarded my welfare check and the one hundred dollars from my Gammie Evelyn and he sent another check for $245 from my security deposit and he didn't say anything about *die welfare slut* on his door—just included a yellow Post-it note that said, *Good luck, Ariel*—so I took Maia's hand and we headed downstairs from Jamie's apartment to the candle shop that advertised the no-fee check cashing.

Two young dykes in flannel shirts kissed in the bus shelter on the corner. Behind them, a poster of a crying toddler with a thought bubble said: *I'm twice as likely not to graduate from high school because you had me as a teen.* Next to that, a black-and-white picture of a young mom emblazoned with the word REJECT in red stared at me. Another picture of a teen mom said DIRTY in red. Another said LOSER. This was the campaign to prevent teen pregnancy that I'd heard about on the AM radio, but the posters seemed more personal than preventative. The girl-moms were too thin, their eye makeup dark and smeared. They didn't quite look at the camera—like they were too ashamed even to make eye contact. The dykes in their flannel shirts kept kissing under the posters, the one pushing her body into the other.

I dreaded Maia learning to read.

I'd been a "reject" long before I got pregnant. I didn't want Maia to think it was her fault.

I had always liked to do whatever was ill-advised.

A bell jingled as I pushed open the door to the botanica. A life-size saint statue greeted us and Maia squinted up at it, unfazed by its bleeding wounds.

The shop smelled familiar, like coconut and sandalwood. Shelves of candles crowded the shotgun space.

A woman in a tight purple leotard top sat behind a glass counter and listened to a customer.

A little girl played with wooden blocks in a back corner.

Maia watched the girl for a long time, then toddled over to join her. Maia's legs were still a little bit bowed like a baby's, but her stride was getting stronger. She was two and a half. I felt proud to be her mother.

I browsed the seven-day candles, eavesdropped on the women's conversation.

The customer had spiked red hair and the word *Chicana* tattooed across her chest in Gothic script. "I need to conjure self-confidence for my sister," she was saying. "I don't even mind if I have to give up some of my own confidence. She was only twelve years old when she got pregnant. She lost all her confidence."

And I did understand that teen pregnancy would feel very different at twelve.

At thirteen.
At fourteen.
At fifteen.
At sixteen.
At seventeen.
At eighteen.
At nineteen.
And none of us needed this shame.

A cat purred against my leg. A small sign on the wall said:

Magick for Beginners
1. Focus on your desire.
2. Practice feeling as if your desire is already reality.
3. Engage physical props to represent the
manifestation of your desire.
(For example, you may light a candle.)
4. Give no fucks about the outcome.

The woman in the purple leotard pulled a large black stone out of her bra, set it on the counter. "All right," she said. "Take this jet stone and every night from the new moon until the full, you're going to speak to it and you're going to fill it with all your love and self-confidence for your sister."

The Chicana-tattoo girl nodded.

"You'll gift your sister with the stone, but there's no need to tell her about all that you've imbued it with. Just tell her it's for good luck—anything to make sure she'll keep it in her home."

"Okay," the girl agreed, pushing her hand through

her spiked hair like she was nervous and confident at the same time.

Her boots made a hollow sound on the floor as she headed out, the door jingling her departure.

The shopkeeper turned to me. "And what, my dear, may I help you with?"

I felt aware of all my skin, like maybe it was made of hot tinfoil. I said, "Oh, I just wanted to see about the free check cashing?" I took the envelope from my pocket and waived it around, all awkward. "Maybe I want to get a candle too?"

"Whatever you like, my dear," the woman said. "No purchase necessary."

I picked up a green candle in a glass cylinder, crept up to the counter, and set it down.

"What would you like to manifest?" the woman asked.

And I said, "I want to go to Mills College in September."

She held up her hand, like *stop*, said, "Cancel, cancel. Repeat after me: I intend to go to Mills College in September."

"I intend to go to Mills College in September," I repeated. "That's what I said."

The woman smiled at me. "No, my dear, you said you *wanted* to go to Mills College in September. Want persists. Intention is swiftly fulfilled."

I nodded. "I *intend* to go to Mills College in September."

She lifted her arms up. "May we be protected in this circle." She took a deep, dramatic breath and exhaled. "To know, to will, to dare, to keep silent."

I thought about that: *To know, to will, to dare—*
those words sounded right and familiar. But *to keep
silent?*

Didn't silence = oppression?

Didn't silence = literary erasure?

Didn't silence = suburban motherhood?

Didn't silence = death?

The woman reached into her bra again and pulled
out a blue stone. "Lapis lazuli," she said. And I wondered how many different stones she kept in there.

She said, "I conjure the spirits of my ancestors who
were locked in mental hospitals for being promiscuous.
They want. They're mad as hell. And they're here now
to provide protection for our bodies and our daughters'
bodies. Strength and beauty." She glanced over at our
daughters, still playing with the wooden blocks. She
said, "Repeat after me: to know, to will, to dare, to keep
silent."

And I nodded into that. "To know, to will, to dare, to
keep silent."

Maybe sometimes silence = necessary stealth.

"We open the circle," she said softly.

Maia and I left the botanica with the cash from our
checks, a spell kit, and a prayer card that pictured Artemis, goddess of the hunt.

The woman in purple had pointed to the meditation.
"Read it aloud to yourself every day."

Artemis, sister, make my aim true.
Give me goals to seek and the
determination to achieve them.

Grant me communion with nature.
Allow me to live surrounded by plants,
animals, and children.
Allow me the strength and wisdom
to be my own mistress.
And empower my ongoing sexual liberation.

That night after Maia fell asleep in our closet, I took scissors and a Sharpie from the drafting table in Jamie's bedroom, cut the collar out of a white T-shirt, and wrote the word REJECT across the front. I cut the collar out of another T-shirt, too, wrote DIRTY. I would own all the words before Maia learned to read. I would impact our surroundings instead of always being impacted.

Then I did as the woman in the purple leotard had instructed me: I drizzled the green candle with wisdom oil, lit it, and set it on the window ledge inside our walk-in closet. I sprinkled Crown of Success powder on my Mills College application and folded it into a green envelope. I rubbed more wisdom oil onto my forehead and whispered, "I intend to go to Mills College in September."

Mills College in September

Across the bay from San Francisco, Mills College was hundred-year-old eucalyptus trees and rolling hills of fresh-cut grass, barbed-wire fences to keep the city out, and the Indigo Girls singing from car stereos.

"Look at what we conjured," I whispered to Maia as I carried the garbage bags full of our things into our on-campus apartment.

"Wikey," she said, all bright moon face.

I read aloud from *Jambalaya*, and we cleansed all the rooms with salt and bay rum, then infused the whole place with our hopes carved into bright candles.

In the little community garden outside, Maia whispered, "Grow!" to the herb plants. "Grow, go."

I picked sprigs of lemon verbena and rosemary.

Inside, I set the herbs in mason-jar vases and made an altar to all the living and dead writers who had visited me in visions.

I had scholarships to cover most of my tuition, and I would tutor statistics students for the economics department as work-study, but I took out student loans for housing and childcare at the Mills education department's "lab" preschool. It seemed like a little bit of a scam that the education students had to pay to teach there and I had to pay for Maia to attend, but they had clean floors and clean wooden toys and childcare is childcare, so, "Bye, bye, Mai, Mai. Have a good day."

She flapped her arms like a butterfly, said, "Too busy now to *bye bye*, Mama."

First day of class and my women's studies professor walked in fast, dropped her briefcase on the metal table, said, "Violence against women is the most pandemic form of violence in the world." She wore a dashiki, her hair in a round seventies Afro.

I opened my notebook and wrote that down: *Violence against women is the most pandemic form of violence in the world.*

Next to her words, I drew the branch of the eucalyptus tree I could see from the classroom window.

At Mills College right then, I felt very far away from violence against women.

My professor said, "Every other form of violence in the world—from bar fights to police brutality to economic injustice to border patrols to international war—is connected to violence against women at home. That's where it begins."

I looked around the room at the other Mills girls.

They slouched in Ralph Lauren.

My breasts ached.

Maybe I shouldn't have worn my homemade REJECT T-shirt.

The professor said, "Raise your hand if you've ever experienced violence."

All the girls raised their hands.

Womyn, I reminded myself. *Mills womyn.*

The professor stared at me. *Had she asked me something?* I wanted to look away, but she'd already seen me see her—to look away now would be even more conspicuous than to hold her gaze. She kept staring.

I didn't blink. And then I did. When I opened my eyes, the professor's eyes were rounder and set just slightly farther apart than they'd been a moment earlier.

I inhaled a quick breath and tried to refocus.

The professor's eyes were the eyes of the deer.

I blinked again.

And now she looked like the professor again. She said, "Never experienced violence?"

Everyone stared at me.

"Oh." I raised my hand quickly. "Of course. I mean. The regular amount. Of violence." I felt panicky. I hadn't meant to *not* raise my hand, but the small violences of my life seemed insignificant compared to police brutality or international war. My tiny mother smashing my head into the wall because I was tinier than she was. Lance standing over me because he felt small, too. The steel blade in my cunt. The man who lived across the street from me in Petaluma who threatened to rip up my welfare check and who I hit—he didn't hit me—the blow that didn't change anything. The red-painted doll.

"The. Regular. Amount. Of. Violence," the professor said slowly. She scanned the room. "The textbooks for this class are *Gender Trouble* by Judith Butler and *Feminist Theory: From Margin to Center* by the eminent bell hooks. If you don't plan on getting them or you don't plan on reading them, today would be an excellent day to drop my class. I realize this is an elective for most of you, but that doesn't mean it's going to be a tea party."

I zipped my notebook into my backpack and headed outside.

On the green expanse, a woman sat behind a plastic folding table.

At the edge of the table, a red Capitalist Bank sign announced:

$50 Bonus to Open Your Checking Account Today.

A squirrel scurried in front of the table, picked up an acorn, and dashed off.

I passed the table once, then circled back. The woman had a pile of temporary checkbooks with that red logo on them. She had a stack of forms. She didn't have a computer where she could look anybody up. On my third pass, she said, "Are you already a Capitalist Bank customer?"

I could feel my heartbeat quicken. I thought of the signature card with my childhood handwriting. I could still picture the blank look on the teller's face back in Petaluma when she told me my account had been closed and the way I'd felt too embarrassed to ask why. "No?" I squeaked.

The woman with the checkbooks and no computer smiled her white teeth. The clear blue sky behind her gleamed like a studio backdrop. "Care to sign up? We've got a fifty-dollar bonus for Mills women today."

I swallowed, nervous. I glanced down to make sure

I wasn't leaking milk onto my REJECT T-shirt. Surely the woman with white teeth would be able to tell I wasn't a real Mills woman. I'd only been accepted to the lesbian college conditionally—pending a passing score on my GED because I'd never finished high school or taken that test. But I said, "Sure, I guess," to the Capitalist Bank woman, and I knelt down on the grass to fill out the form. I felt the damp of the lawn on my knees as it seeped through my jeans. I breathed in deep, trying to fill my lungs with the air of entitlement. I imagined my falcon flying into Mills College ahead of me on Artemis's arrow—not Sylvia Plath's. *Yes,* I told myself, *I have as much right to be here as the squirrels and the rich girls.*

The woman with white teeth handed me a temporary checkbook like it was no big deal—like anybody could have a bank account just for asking. "You've already got fifty dollars in there," she smiled, and I felt a pang of sadness in my throat at the truth that Capitalist Bank took money from the workers and the welfare moms of Petaluma in 10 percent and 20 percent check-cashing fees on the other side of the river and gave it to the rich girls at Mills College for free.

I stuck the checkbook in the pocket of my backpack and shrugged like, *Yeah, no big deal.* I said, "Thanks," but I was careful to say it all blasé so the woman with white teeth wouldn't think I didn't expect to have a bank account, didn't expect to be given money.

In the Mills College bookstore, I set the red paperback copy of *Feminist Theory: From Margin to Center* on the counter, wrote a check for $8.81.

Next to the register, a photograph of a wide-eyed woman holding a wide-eyed baby stared up at me from a tin can. A sign above the picture said: "Donate your change to help women in poverty." I peered into that can of quarters and nickels and wondered how the rich girls felt when they dropped in maybe fifty cents from their free fifty dollars to help the women in poverty.

Behind the bookstore, at the end of a flower-lined path, education students doted on Maia at the lab preschool.

"No, Mama," she said to me when I stepped inside. "I too busy go home."

"Are you the nanny?" one of the education students asked, smiling. She wore a clean paisley shirt.

"No, I'm her mom. That's why she calls me Mama."

The clean one laughed. "Oh! Well, your daughter is the most *poised* three-year-old I've ever met in my life."

"Thanks," I said. "She's only two and a half." But I liked the clean teacher in her clean paisley shirt.

I said, "It's time to go home, Mai, Mai. You can come back tomorrow."

"Promise come back?"

"Promise, baby."

We walked across all that green toward our apartment, counting our steps and listening to the birds chirp their banking-class songs from the trees of Mills College. Orchids and petunias pressed themselves up through the topsoil and grew magic-fast and bloomed.

"You're *poised*," I told Maia.

"Look," she said, pointing up.

And there in a high branch of a London planetree perched our old friend, the red-winged blackbird.

I sang up to her, "What says you, red-winged blackbird?"

"Says you," Maia echoed.

And the bird tilted her head to the side and she sang back down to us, "Isn't it nice to sneak back into the banking class?"

Evening and the full harvest moon shone through tall eucalyptus trees outside the picture window of our new apartment.

Then a blast of garage music from the building across the driveway.

I peered out.

A girl with a crew cut and a big pregnant belly danced on the cement steps of her front porch. She held a toddler on her hip. An older kid stood next to her, licking a popsicle. The pregnant girl yelled the lyrics of her music: "I'm a *teen*age *wel*fare mother!"

I stared at the girl, kind of stunned.

"Hey," she called over to me. "Did you just move in here?"

"Yeah," I called back. "I just transferred here. What are you listening to?"

The sudden sound of gunfire from the other side of the fence made all the birds take flight.

"Little Red Car Wreck!" the girl-mom yelled as wings and beaks darted for cover. She gestured in the direction the shots had come from. "Don't worry," she said, "you'll get used to all the juxtapositions here."

"Juxtapositions," I whispered to myself. That was probably going to be on the GED.

*

"Living as we did—on the edge—we developed a particular way of seeing reality," I read to Maia from the bell hooks feminist-theory book as she eased into sleep. "We looked both from the outside in and from the inside out. We focused our attention on the center as well as on the margin. We understood both. This mode of seeing reminded us of the existence of a whole universe, a main body made up of both margin and center. Our survival depended on an ongoing public awareness of the separation between margin and center and an ongoing private acknowledgment that we were a necessary, vital part of that whole."

I felt tired, and Maia was asleep now, but I kept reading.

"Women, even the most oppressed among us, do exercise power." I whispered in Maia's ear: "Women need to know that they can reject the powerful's definition of their reality—that they can do so even if they are poor, exploited, or trapped in oppressive circumstances. They need to know that the exercise of this basic personal power is an act of resistance and strength."

I got out of bed. I was still wearing my homemade REJECT T-shirt, and now I took it off and added new words with my Sharpie so it said,

REJECT
their definitions of your reality

I liked that you could read it a couple of different ways.

The sudden sound of glass shattering surprised me.

— 185 —

The baby cried out in her sleep.

I put my T-shirt back on fast.

Lance's fist came through the glass first, then the thick of his forearm. A shard of my door sliced into him and blood dripped onto my new apartment carpet.

"Jesus Christ, Lance, that's not how you open a door." I picked up the phone to dial 911.

"You're ringing the bloody pigs?" Lance slurred.

"Yes, I'm calling the pigs." I'd had it. Calling 911 seemed like the empowered thing to do, the feminist thing to do.

The operator was all calm. "Nine-one-one, what's your emergency?"

"My ex just broke the window pane in my door. He's reaching in and unlocking it. He's coming into the house. He's coming toward me now." I felt that familiar sense of calm pragmatism that can cloak fear.

Lance marched right up to me, grabbed the phone cord, and pulled it out of the wall. He hadn't hit me since a long time ago—before the baby—but my cheek-bone remembered the shape of his fist and ached from the memory.

The notes from my women's studies class were penciled graffiti in my notebook on the table: *Violence against women is the most pandemic form of violence in the world.*

Lance puffed his body up and clenched his fists.

"You're such an asshole," I said as I managed to get the plug back into the wall.

"I trust you're not talking to me," the 911 operator said, "but it sounds like you might be right about him."

Now a Mills College security guard appeared in my open doorway, and Lance deflated himself and lit a cigarette and sauntered over to talk to the guard man-to-man, like, *Can you believe this hysterical bitch called the pigs on me over nothing?*

My calm pragmatism evaporated. I started breathing too fast even though I knew it only made me look the part of the hysterical bitch. I felt panicky and I couldn't stop the feeling. I needed the cops to believe that Lance was being aggressive, that I wasn't just crazy, that I had been in danger, possibly, when I called, that I wasn't just overreacting because I'd been reading bell hooks, but the harder I breathed, the less sure I was of myself. I couldn't stop my arms from shaking. I couldn't stop my jaw from clenching.

Maia toddled out into the living room, called, "Dada?" to the doorway. She didn't seem afraid, and my chest ached with the reality that this was a kind of normal for her. She started to hum and play with her witch doll.

Now an Oakland patrol car threw red lights into all the apartment windows in the family-housing complex, and my skin stung with embarrassment to be making this huge scene the first week of classes at Mills College.

Two Oakland cops got out of their car, and they both walked over to talk to Lance and the security guard first. Then just the female cop stepped up to my door, all butch swagger, and I thought she was kind of hot, but then she opened her mouth and her voice demurred, "So, you and your husband got in a fight?"

Her badge said *Jones.*

"He's not my husband," I said. "He's not even supposed to be here. I didn't invite him."

She inspected my broken glass.

"He smashed the door," I said fast. It seemed so obviously problematic and illegal that he was here. Maybe *I* was just now learning about boundaries and violence against women, but surely the cops were better versed. *Shouldn't they be? If violence against women was the most pandemic form of violence in the world?*

"He says you're married, ma'am," the male cop said as he walked up, and he pointed to Maia like, *Did I think I could pull one over on them?* "He says he forgot his key, ma'am. He thought you were asleep when you didn't answer the door, so . . ."

I felt crazy. This was my apartment. My name was on the student lease. This was a women's college. bell hooks was old and people referred to her as "the eminent bell hooks."

"Do you have a divorce decree?" Jones tried, like that was the thing that would substantiate my story.

I shook my head. I waved my hands around in the dark. I mean, of course I didn't have a fucking divorce decree. "I'm not married," I said again. "We're not married. We were never married. So we're not divorced."

Jones looked concerned but bewildered, too, like she'd never met anyone who wasn't married before, which didn't make any sense. I mean, it was 1992. *Had I hallucinated the entire decade of the 1970s in the Bay Area when I was a kid?* No one's parents were married. And the 1980s with all the women in their blue power suits and Reeboks with their *Ms.* magazine subscriptions? Not everyone got married. A lot of people actually considered it kind of weird to get married—and god forbid marry young. I mean, marriage meant you were a hillbilly, *didn't it?* Marriage meant you were either a hillbilly or a Mormon, I was sure of it.

Jones said, "You can get a restraining order, ma'am. If you don't want your husband in your house." And I felt politically embarrassed that I'd thought she was hot, even for a second. Jones was not hot. Jones was not at all hot.

"All right," I breathed. Of course it was ridiculous that I needed a court order to make it not all right for someone to show up and break my door whenever he pleased, but all right. "All right," I said.

I watched Lance as he wandered away, chatting with the Mills College security guard like the two of them might grab a beer now.

Was I crazy?

Was I this hysterical bitch?

After they'd gone, I sat on our cement porch in the late summer moonlight and nursed Maia back to sleep.

The girl-mom with the crew cut from the apartment across the driveway called over to me: "I'm glad I'm not the only one with some trashy-ass family that somehow always involves the cops by 8:00 p.m."

I liked her already.

"My name's Lola," she called over.

"I'm Ariel," I called back. And I felt something like relief.

Lola said, "You should bring your daughter over to meet my kids tomorrow. Bring coffee if you have any?"

"All right." Yes, I had coffee. Café Bustelo would be my social capital.

I carried Maia back to our mattress for the night, snuggled next to her, and kept reading the bell hooks. Morning sunlight seeped into our room. *Did I have class today? Could it be Saturday?*

I whisper-read to Maia, "The formation of an oppositional world view is necessary for feminist struggle. This means that the world we have most intimately known, the world in which we feel 'safe' (even if such feelings are based on illusions), must be radically changed."

I knew that bell hooks meant that I had to change too.

In what ways was I serving the oppressor?

I pulled on my jeans, wandered sleepy into the kitchen, grabbed my yellow can of Bustelo coffee from the counter, said, "C'mon, baby," and Maia and I headed across the driveway to meet the other half of our little subculture.

Don't Be Surprised
When Your Magic Works

It seemed to me that Lola embodied everything I didn't: fat and happy and brazen and unapologetic about everything including the whole sexed-up single-mom thing. She said, "I'm trying to recruit as many people as possible to eat my pussy while I'm pregnant. I hypothesize that if I come to orgasm at least once every day, my baby will be born enlightened. Wouldn't that be cool? Even if I can't prove my theory, I get to *come* every day. What do you think?"

I sipped my coffee. "I think it sounds like a worthy hypothesis."

"No!" Lola howled. "What do you think about eating my pussy?"

I blushed, glanced over at Maia and the other kids as they built a kingdom out of textbooks and pots and pans across Lola's carpeted living room. None of them seemed to be listening to our conversation, *but still. Were all the girls at Mills this forward? When did Lola even have time for sex?* One kid felt like a lot to me, but here Lola had two kids and a third on the way and she was recruiting new people to eat her pussy every day? Like, *Was she having a manic episode?*

She said, "What's your family doing for Halloween?" And I thought she meant my parents, so I said,

"My mom usually dresses up the human skeleton she keeps in the closet and gives out apples with fake razor blades in them." But Lola said, "No, I mean you and Maia—your family." And right then I kind of choked up because no one had ever referred to Maia and me as a family before. Not ever.

Had I myself accepted our illegitimacy as a premise?

Lola said, "Explain to me this: women like you and me—especially Latina women like me—we're seen as procreating at dangerous rates, but now they're calling black men and Latino men 'endangered species.'" She gestured toward her kids. "It's racist, right?"

I nodded. "Double racist."

"Thank you," she said. "My mother was Puerto Rican and my dad's Italian and Okie and my son Lyle's mixed with African American, obviously, but Leena's dad was white so she doesn't even look Latina." Lola leaned back in her chair, rubbed her huge belly, said, "I planned to stop at two kids but my mom died last year, so I couldn't very well abort. I mean, what if this is my mother's soul-baby? You never know. Not that I'm against abortion. I've had one. It's not a tragedy not to get a body." Lola stood up fast. "Ariel?"

"Yes, Lola?"

"Do you love Diane di Prima?"

Did I love Diane di Prima? I wracked my brain, but the name only rang a vague bell. "The beatnik?"

Lola laughed again. "Of course the beatnik! And so much more! The *poet!*" She grabbed a copy of *Revolutionary Letters* from a small built-in cupboard that also held Virgin of Guadalupe statues and pictures of her kids as babies. She started reading out loud: "Left to themselves people grow their hair. Left to themselves they take off their shoes. Left to themselves they make love, sleep easily, share blankets, dope & children. They are not lazy or afraid. They plant seeds, they smile, they speak to one another." She flipped pages, read more, "As you learn the magic, learn to believe it. Don't be 'surprised' when it works, you undercut your power." Lola looked up at me. "You're a *bruja*, right?"

I didn't know what to say.

"A witch?" she almost yelled. "I saw you gathering the rosemary and lemon verbena from the community garden when you first moved in. And I saw the black cat you sneaked in." Lola was silent for a moment and then her face started to fall and I didn't want to disappoint her.

I'd picked those herbs for the altar mostly because they smelled good, but I knew that rosemary was used for protection and lemon verbena for new starts, so I said, "Maybe?" I still didn't know how Maia had conjured up Luna.

Lola rubbed her hands together. "Thank goddess. I want to learn to be a *bruja* too."

I corrected her, "I *intend* to learn to be a *bruja* too."

Maia climbed onto my lap. "*Bruja*."

And Lola repeated after me, "I *intend* to learn to be a *bruja*."

Yes, we would now speak only in foregone conclusions.

White-Lady Feminism 101

Bring a mirror.

Poor Little Male Violence

A lone protester dressed in black jeans and a black T-shirt stood outside the Alameda County court building holding a sign that read, "This is a misogynist institution." But I'd only seen the word *misogynist* in Adrienne Rich books and the witch's zine and I didn't think much about the lone protester.

Inside, giant black moths fluttered their wings against the white walls and snakes slithered in corners and I pretended not to notice because surely only crazy people noticed all those giant moths and snakes in the Alameda County court building.

A woman behind bulletproof glass asked me quick questions: "Civil restraining order or domestic violence, ma'am?" She had hearts airbrushed onto her acrylic nails.

"Civil, I think? He doesn't live with us."

"How do you know him, ma'am?"

"He's my daughter's father."

"That's domestic violence, ma'am. That's family law."

"Oh, all right. Thanks."

Another corridor. Flickering lights. The sound of staplers. *Click. Click.* More women behind glass. The fluttering of moths. The tearing of wings. The blood of the moths.

I said, "I need a domestic-violence restraining order."

"Are you married, ma'am?"

"No."

"Your boyfriend?"

"No. He's my daughter's father."

"Is there already a court order for custody?"

"No."

"All right. You need to file for a temporary restraining order." *Click. Click.* "But you'll also have to file a complaint to establish a parental relationship with this form." *Click. Click.* "That'll take care of the question of custody too. And visitation." *Click. Click.*

"My daughter lives with me."

"Yes, ma'am. That's fine. You still need to file the paperwork. If you want to keep yourself and your daughter safe, if you want a restraining order, you'll need to file all the paperwork. Right now he can take her away whenever he wants and you wouldn't have any right to see her." The woman with airbrushed nails stared at me. "You'd never see your daughter again."

"What?"

"Fill out all the paperwork, ma'am."

"Oh, all right. Thanks."

"Then he'll have to stay a hundred yards away from you."

"Okay, thanks." I filled out the paperwork.

*

In a wood-paneled courtroom, women stood as a short clerk with tremendous breasts called out our names.

"Letisha Thomas."

"Here."

"Colette Woo."

"Here."

"Harmony Nguyen."

"Here."

"Reina Hernandez."

"Here."

"Ariel Gore."

"Here."

"All rise," the clerk sang, like she was in some kind of opera.

The judge marched in and took his seat, not even looking up to make sure we'd all stood in deference. He shook his bald white head at the stack of papers in front of him, said, "Everyone's abused?" like he was pretty skeptical about that.

Hadn't he been to college? Didn't he—a family-court judge of all people—know that violence against women was the most pandemic form of violence in the world? The cops hadn't understood, but surely one needed more education to be a judge? What did he mean by that, anyway, everyone's abused? I wanted to raise my hand and say, *Yes, your honor. Over a million women are abused by their partners each year. Two out of three female homicides are committed by lovers or close family members. Statistically speaking, we're safer in dark alleys than we are in our own homes,* but I stayed quiet.

The judge stamped my restraining order. *Click. Click.*

*

That afternoon, I picked Maia up from the campus

lab preschool, and we headed home to our apartment, counting clouds.

Lola sat with one of her kids on their cement steps. "Hey," she said as we walked up. "Come over for coffee?"

"Sure," I smiled, all hopeful.

But as I sat at Lola's little kitchen table listening to Ani DiFranco and waiting for the water to boil, I showed her the paperwork from the court with the temporary restraining order. I'd done what the cops had told me to do. I'd done the feminist thing. I didn't know why they'd scheduled a second court date in a month.

Lola covered her mouth as she paged through the documents. "Oh my goddess," she whispered. "You're fucked."

"What is it?"

Lola shook her head. "Your restraining order triggered a complaint to establish a parental relationship." She measured coffee from my yellow can.

"What does it mean?"

"It means you're legally bound to him now," she said. "Until Maia's eighteen. As long as you both shall live. You're bound."

"Can I undo it?"

Lola shook her head. "I don't know. They're not even going to care that he's an illegal alien because he's white. You need a lawyer." And she pointed to all the words in those papers that might as well have said:

Come in, male violence.

Poor little angry, hurt boy left out in the cold.

Poor little male violence—

You can climb my hair.

Queen of the Sea

I woke before sunrise to the sound of singing. I felt disoriented and scrambled from the mattress on the floor to my bedroom window. Outside, under the morning moon, a woman with two long braids sang what sounded like an old fishing song. She sang, *"The herring is the queen of the sea, the herring is the fish for me."*

Was it a song about herring?

She sang, *"Herring's eyes, puddings and pies."*

Was it a song about what to do with all the parts of a herring?

She kept singing.

I grabbed a pair of jeans from the floor next to the mattress and pulled them on, pulled a sweatshirt on over my T-shirt. I nudged Maia awake, and she rubbed her eyes and followed me through the living room and outside.

The singing woman kept singing, but she turned away from us and started walking, so I took Maia's sweaty hand in mine and we followed the singing woman as she walked and sang down the hill and away from Mills College. She sang, *"What'll we do with the herring's heads? We'll make 'em all into loaves of bread!"*

At the edge of campus, the singing woman easily scaled the fence, and Maia and I followed her. I ripped the skin near my elbow on the barbed wire as I lifted Maia's body to clear it, but the hurt felt fine. On the far side, I jumped the last few yards onto a sidewalk. "Jump," I called up to Maia, and she jumped into my arms and laughed.

She wore her dinosaur pajamas, and I wondered how much longer she'd trust in a catch like that.

We followed the singing woman as she sang, *"Oh, what'll we do with the herring's fins? We'll make them all into needles and pins."*

Urban jasmine vined up chain-link fences along our way, and morning glory clung to the freeway underpasses.

The singing woman stopped suddenly, so we stopped too. I looked up to gray-black graffiti spray-painted across a concrete wall:

We are concerned that you are learning empowerment without self-preservation.

I blinked. And when I glanced back up to the singing woman, she'd turned a silvery steel-blue color.

Maia opened her eyes wide. "Is she a mermaid, Mama?"

The singing woman knelt down at the edge of the street, and with her human hands she lifted the iron grate from a storm drain. She wriggled her feet into the hole and sat on the edge. She started singing again, more slowly this time: *"The herring is the queen of the sea, the herring is the fish for me."* As she sang, she began to grow scales, and her arms became fins, and her eyes became round, and she puckered her blue lips, and she slipped down into the storm drain still singing: *"The herring is the queen of the sea, the herring is the fish for me . . ."*

I looked back up at the graffiti.

We are concerned that you are learning empowerment without self-preservation.

Sugar on My Tongue

Right hand red. Left foot blue. Maia stretched under me and across the Twister board. I reached over her, then heard the hard knock on the door and had to untangle myself.

Early evening and Lola looked serious, pulled her flannel shirt around her shoulders. "I'm in labor," she said, "but I can't miss this psych midterm. Can you come over and watch Lyle and Leena for a couple hours?"

"Of course."

"Play with the kid?" Maia yelled, and she buzzed into our room to change into her dinosaur pajamas.

"My mom said we didn't have to go to sleep," Leena announced as soon as Lola let the door shut behind her. Leena's blond hair was tangled, with a blue barrette holding it back from her forehead. "No matter what happens, we don't have to sleep."

I'd never heard Leena talk before, and I liked her firm stance.

"We're listening to Talking Heads," she said, and she pushed play.

So we sat on the couch, the two of us, listening to

Talking Heads while Maia hummed the herring song and she and Lyle decorated the living room with toilet-paper streamers.

"Do you wanna make snow angels in the carpet?" I asked Leena.

So that's what we were doing—making snow angels in the carpet—when there was a knock at the door. I got up and looked through the peephole in the front door, saw two men I'd never seen before. I lifted Leena to let her look. "Do you know them?"

Leena nodded. "Good guys."

So I opened the door.

The taller man had long hair. "I'm Piedro?" He said it like I might know that name.

I shrugged.

"I'm Lola's lover?"

And I nodded.

"I'm the baby's father," he said, and he pointed to the man standing next to him. "And this is my husband, Matthew."

I shook each of their hands.

"Piedro!" Lyle called from the back of the living room, and he rushed up to hug him.

"My mom's not back from her midterm yet," Leena told them.

Matthew held up a box of raspberry-leaf tea and a six-pack of Corona. "We brought these for the labor."

"So, come on in."

It was maybe a half an hour later when Lola burst back in, yelling, "Who's a warrior goddess!" She raised a fist, rushed into the kitchen, and lifted up her skirt as her water broke onto the linoleum.

"Holy shit, Lola!"

"*You're* a warrior goddess," Piedro said, all smitten. Lola took a deep, dramatic breath, put a Nirvana tape in, then shook her head. "Probably Tracy Chapman's better right now."

Lola called her midwife and called her again on speakerphone from the kitchen table, but she just kept getting an answering machine with an outgoing message that said, "Be here now."

Lola moaned and squatted.

"I should call 911," I said, "just in case."

"Don't call the fucking pigs," Lola cried. "I'm okay."

I glanced at Piedro and Matthew, like maybe they knew how this was supposed to go, but they didn't give me any cues. I believed in Lola—she'd already had two kids—but I was scared too. Leena stood with me, wide-eyed. She dug her little fingers into my arm as Lyle and Maia danced to the music.

Lola screamed suddenly.

And then Leena was the one to pick up the phone. "My mom's having a baby," she blurted into the dial tone, and just then I saw the crown of a head and the tips of shoulders and Lola reached inside of herself and pulled—crown to forehead, forehead to squished-shut eyes, squished-shut eyes to scrunched nose. Now Piedro yelled, too, and stumbled toward Lola to catch the baby.

Lola screamed and pulled and pushed, blood and amniotic fluid.

Leena gasped, all anxiety, and bit my arm hard. "Put on Talking Heads," Lyle pleaded, like Talking Heads would make Leena okay, but everything was chaos for the moment.

"It's all right, baby," I promised Leena and
then,
miraculously,
it was.

Lola lay on the couch with the baby girl against her chest.

"It's okay," I said again to Leena.

"It's okay," Lyle said too.

"It's okay," Maia whispered.

"'Sugar on My Tongue'?" Leena asked softly.

And I turned down Tracy Chapman and I cued up Talking Heads and now Lola's midwife stood in the doorway, breathless. "Oh my goddess," she said. "I got on the bus as soon as I heard your first message."

Lola exhaled and started crying just then, like she'd saved up all her anxiety until now. "You told me the third one comes fast," she said. "I should have called you before my midterm started."

The midwife sighed and smiled at that. "Indeed."

Lola sat up suddenly. "Can someone go get us some chicken? I have money. It's in the envelope in *This Kind of Bird Flies Backward*."

I pulled the Diane di Prima book from the shelf, and sure enough, a little wrinkled envelope inside held a pile of wrinkled fives, like Lola had been saving up for this day a long time. I buckled all the kids into the car and we headed off, leaving Lola and her lover and her lover's husband and the baby and the midwife to rest, and Leena and I sang "Sugar on My Tongue" all the way to Home of Chicken and Waffles and back again, and Leena grinned, a gleam in her eye, and said, "Whenever my mom has a baby, we don't have to sleep at all."

We Were Meant to Be Witches

In February of my senior year, Bill Clinton signed "Don't ask, don't tell."

It would be another couple of years before he dismantled welfare rights while he had sex with his intern and then tried to redefine sex to exclude cocksucking and rimming.

The woman who worked at Mama Bear's bookstore on Telegraph Avenue in Oakland said, "Whatever you do, don't tell 'em you're a lesbian." She wore a button that said "girl riot" and kept her straight hair in pigtails. Her look confused me because I thought we were all supposed to be women and womyn and not girls, but I tried to be cool with it. *Like, whatever.*

I'd placed a self-help family-law book on the counter, and I'd had three espressos, too, so I blabbed my problem: "I made a mistake. I filed for a restraining order. That triggered a family-court hearing for custody. He never even wanted custody."

The girl sucked in her cheeks. "I don't have custody of my kids, okay? Just don't tell them how you identify."

I nodded fast. "Okay." I didn't quite know what she meant by "identify," but I knew I wanted to identify as a mother who had custody of her child.

I wasn't having sex with anyone, anyway.

It seemed easy enough.

"I'm not kidding," the riot woman said.

And I nodded. "I understand."

I would not ask. I would not tell.

*

Lance sauntered into the family-court mediation meeting late, looking like Sid Vicious in his black jeans and black leather jacket, and I rolled my eyes.

Way back before the baby, we'd bonded on the rooftop of a squat in Amsterdam over a hash cigarette and an affinity for the Clash and A. S. Neill, but that felt like a random memory that shouldn't have led anywhere.

Lola said we're all attracted to people who remind us of our families of origin. Lance was crazy like my dad, drunk like my Gammie Evelyn, violent like my mom, and muscular like my stepdad. I wondered if I would ever attract a brighter reflection of my family: someone brilliant like my dad, generous like my Gammie Evelyn, artistic like my mom, and Zen like my stepdad.

The mediator had dark curly hair like mine, said, "All right, we're here to talk about custody and visitation." She cleared her throat, paged through the papers on her desk. "For, um, *Me-ah?* Mia is it?"

Lance leaned back in his chair like he was too cool for any of this. He said, "I don't want bloody custody. I haven't got anyplace for her to sleep."

That much was true. He lived part-time at the home where he worked as a caregiver and crashed the other nights with his sometimes girlfriend at her makeshift loft in an artist's warehouse.

"Well," the mediator snapped at him, not even looking at me, "if neither of you is fit to parent, we can put Mia in foster care."

I felt my throat close.

Lance squinted, like he was as confused as I was now. He gestured toward me. "What's wrong with 'er? She's 'er muther."

"Children need fathers," the mediator said flatly. "The standard is fifty-fifty joint custody after a divorce."

"We weren't married," I tried to say, but it came out in a whisper.

Lance's face flushed. "We weren't some bloody Ozzie and Harriet family you havta mend."

"We need to work out a schedule," the mediator said. "A week on, a week off?"

I tried to picture it. Maia would stay home with me for a week and then where? How would I get her to the lab preschool in the mornings if she had to stay someplace with him?

Lance slammed his fist on the desk fast and hard. "I said I haven't got a place for her." He looked around the room like he'd just noticed it didn't have any windows. "Ariel's a bloody good mother," he said, almost desperate.

Lance thought I was a bloody good mother?

The mediator shook her head. "I'm going to recommend anger management for you, sir."

I watched Lance as he kept talking fast under the

fluorescent lights in that office, and my heart felt oddly caught in my lungs. Lance had just been a fist through glass to me for years—at least since the baby—and here he was defending my honor. Or maybe it was just that we were both so fundamentally alienated from the idealized notion of the nuclear family that we'd finally found something in common. He'd grown up in foster care after his artist single mother committed suicide.

The mediator took a deep breath, looked at me for the first time. She was maybe forty. She didn't wear any makeup.

I wondered if she was a dyke. I wanted to smooth moisturizer under her eyes.

She said, "Mrs. Gore, I'd like to speak with your husband privately for a few moments."

And that's when my heart sank back to where it belonged. "We aren't married," I managed as I stood up to leave. Right then I felt very confused. I was proud of Lance for trying to explain a world beyond the nuclear family to our maybe-dyke mediator, but I felt dread, too. The hall where I waited could have been a court hall or a school hall or a hospital hall—its institutional white walls and white floor and bright white lights reflected off of each other, dizzying me with white. I wanted a cigarette so badly my gums hurt. I'd given myself a red manicure, trying to look like I had my shit together, but now I bit my fingernails until they bled and I kept biting, savoring the salty taste of my own flesh.

Finally the door to the mediator's office inched open. A voice: "Mrs. Gore?"

By the time I sat back down in that mediator's office, Lance had fallen quiet. He had tears in his brown eyes.

The mediator said, "Lance, is there something you want to say to Ariel?"

I tasted copper and swallowed hard. The mediator hadn't had him for long, but I knew he was easy to manipulate.

"Maybe Maia deserves a father," Lance said to me, and he choked back tears as he said it. "I never had a father."

The mediator nodded at him and then at me. "I'm going to recommend the judge continue this case. Your husband has agreed to anger management and parenting classes. We'll revisit the question of custody and visitation in thirty days."

The fluorescent light beat down on me like a terrible chemical sun.

*

Every Wednesday after that, the mediator or a social worker or the court-appointed psychologist met Lance in the white hallway and told him that if he just got sober, that if he just got his green card, that if he just got a steady job, that if he just completed the anger-management series or the parenting classes already, well, he could be a wonderful father.

They told him children need fathers.

Over and over again, they told him children need fathers.

He cried and cracked his knuckles.

Outside, I smoked cigarettes and crushed the burning cherries into my wrists.

*

From the Mills College library, I checked out *The Poetics of Space* by Gaston Bachelard and read it cover to cover.

What are the poetics of a closet, Gaston Bachelard?

At first I felt frustrated that Gaston didn't mention closets in that book. (Aren't books shaped exactly like closets? Deceptively simple doors shielding secrets.) But then I thought about the apartment where I lived in Spain with Lance and Jamie before I was pregnant and I remembered it didn't have a closet, exactly. I thought about the apartment where I lived in Italy with Lance when I was pregnant and I remembered it didn't have a closet, exactly. Gaston's place in Paris probably didn't have a closet either. Europeans used armoires and wardrobes instead of closets. By *wardrobe*, I decided, Gaston meant *closet*.

He wrote, "Does there exist a single dreamer of words who does not respond to the word *wardrobe*?"

I wanted to be a dreamer of words.

I would respond to the word *closet*.

Gaston wrote, *The real wardrobe is not an everyday piece of furniture. It is not opened every day, and so, like a heart that confides in no one, the key is not on the door.*

I would confide in no one. I would not leave the key on the door.

I read to Maia from our new library book: "Sometimes the house of the future is better built, lighter and larger than all the houses of the past, so that the image of the dream house is opposed to that of the childhood home."

Maia was three years old.

I wondered if she would ever have a childhood home.

I wondered what would happen to us.

She said, "House of the future," all matter-of-fact, like a foregone conclusion.

I kept reading to her. "Maybe it is a good thing for us to keep a few dreams of a house that we shall live in later, always later, so much later, in fact, that we shall not have time to achieve it. For a house that was final, one that stood in symmetrical relation to the house we were born in, would lead to thoughts—serious, sad thoughts—and not to dreams. It is better to live in a state of impermanence than in one of finality."

Getting it together to have a partner and a kid at the same time had been marketed to us as finality, as "happily ever after," but what if our lives don't peak at "happily ever," and instead become a series of impermanent scenes and memories?

After Maia fell asleep, I kept reading: "In the wardrobe there exists a center of order that protects the entire house against uncurbed disorder. Here order reigns, or rather, this is the reign of order. Order is not merely geometrical; it can also remember the family history."

Could my closet be the order that protected us?
Could my closet symbolize refuge instead of silence?
Could my closet become my little clubhouse of resistance?
Could my closet remember our family history?
Could my closet someday become my book?

My closet in our apartment at Mills College was wide and shallow, with sliding mirror doors. Sometimes I sat on the floor inside that closet and I rolled the door back and forth on its rollers just to listen to the sound.
My wardrobe.

Gaston Bachelard quoted Colette Wartz, saying,
Orderliness. Harmony.
Piles of sheets in the wardrobe
Lavender in the linen.
Maybe I would fill my closet with lavender.

I had been told many times by now what I was, but it occurred to me that I'd never articulated any identity for myself.
I loved the soft mouths of my lovers.
I was turned on by masculinity in people who had been socialized as girls.
I was attracted to misfits and addicts and to people who were sometimes mean to themselves and to each other.
I was pretty sure I'd never kissed anyone who thought the world was terrific.

I bought fresh paint for my closet from a guy on the corner outside the paint shop on Forty-Second and

Telegraph Avenue. He had one can of rosy purple and one can of orange.

As I painted, I knew the chemicals would contribute to whatever killed me someday, but I liked the way that inhaling the paint made me feel less afraid.

I put a magazine rack in my closet for *off our backs* and *On Our Backs*. I put a little bookshelf in my closet, too, for Adrienne Rich and June Jordan and Judith Butler and Ntozake Shange and Leslie Feinberg.

I put a reading lamp in my closet.

In *Gender Trouble*, Judith Butler said: *If to become a lesbian is an act, a leave-taking of heterosexuality, a self-naming that contests the compulsory meanings of heterosexuality's women and men, what is to keep the name of lesbian from becoming an equally compulsory category? What qualifies as a lesbian? Does anyone know?*

For Judith Butler, gender was always a kind of performance.

Did she know that motherhood was performance too?

My mother hated me on sight, but it was nothing personal. She hated herself too.

I loved my daughter instinctively, but I couldn't bend myself into the definitions of *mother* I'd been handed. Even if I hadn't been unwed and too young to be invited to the performance, I don't think I could have pulled it off—the self-effacing. I needed magic instead and a new definition of maternal love that allowed for us both to thrive.

I read *Sassafrass, Cypress & Indigo* and I liked the

way that daughterhood didn't strangle motherhood in that book, and I told myself I'd write a story as beautiful as that someday and I'd include spells in my book just like Ntozake Shange did and I thought that would be the coolest thing.

I would become a woman who knew her magic.

From my closet at Mills College, I heard women chanting outside, the sound of their voices coming closer. They were on campus. They shouted, "Take back the night!"

Maia had already fallen asleep.

I never went to a Take Back the Night march.

I am the space where I am, Gaston Bachelard wrote.

I am this closet, painted rosy purple and orange.

I am this book, which is not entirely factual.

*

From the Mills College library, I checked out *The Epistemology of the Closet* by Eve Kosofsky Sedgwick, but I couldn't read that one to Maia, just like I couldn't read her most of *Gender Trouble*, for fear she'd repeat some of the words to the family court-appointed psychologist we were supposed to meet next week and, in doing so, out me and land herself in foster care.

I was trying to learn self-preservation.

I read to myself, "There are remarkably few of even the most openly gay people who are not deliberately in the closet with someone personally or economically or institutionally important to them. Furthermore, the deadly elasticity of heterosexist presumption means that, like Wendy in *Peter Pan*, people find new walls springing up around them even as they drowse." I opened my eyes and watched the walls of my closet spring up high like the walls of a tower.

"Read to me, Mama," Maia called to me from our bed, sleepy, and as I crept out of the closet I knew she was expecting Audre Lorde or bell hooks, but I reached over and grabbed the copy of *Rapunzel* my mother had bought for us back in Petaluma.

I read to her, "Once upon a time . . ."

"Say 'Rapunzel,'" Maia laughed when I read.

I said, "Rapunzel!"

"Say 'Rapunzel' again!" She laughed, like the word itself delighted her.

"Rapunzel!"

Maia unfurled her hair like I might climb it.

And it occurred to me that fairy tales are a kind of grooming.

I played along, but I couldn't help crying, too, and I couldn't help covering my face to pretend I wasn't crying for all the ways I knew we would have to mold ourselves into princesses even though I knew perfectly well we were meant to be witches.

I kept reading from the book as Maia fell back asleep. When she closed her eyes I whispered, "Don't forget when we were witches."

And without opening her eyes, she whispered back, "We were witches."

Children Need Fathers

I am curly headed and freckle faced, flat chested and knobby kneed; I am safe in my body.

There's just one rule my mother has given me for when I visit my Gammie and Grandpa Gore in their little yellow house on Carmel Beach: "When they take you out to the country club, order the most expensive thing on the menu."

My Gammie Gore is sensible slacks, short gray hair, and round glasses.

My grandpa's leg makes a quick mechanical exhaling sound when it bends.

My grandparents are gin and tonic at five o'clock, the *Wall Street Journal* in the morning.

Crab Louie is the most expensive thing on the menu at the country club.

From every room in my grandparents' little yellow house, early in the morning, I can hear the ocean. But when my Gammie wakes up, and after my grandpa takes his bath with his handheld showerhead and after he hops back across the hall to put on his leg, the televisions begin to turn on, one by one—one in every room—and pretty soon you can't hear the ocean at all, and it's time for raisin bran with skim milk and a grapefruit cut in half, neatly segmented with my grandmother's curved little knife.

Midmorning, I creep down from my grandparents' soft-carpeted yellow house to the basement apartment where my father lives, and here there are just two more rules whispered after the word *schizophrenia*: "Don't get in the car with him; don't leave the beach with him."

Time ago, my father soaked his draft card in blood, dropped out of UC Berkeley, put six tabs of acid on his tongue, and howled like Allen Ginsberg across America from Big Sur, California, to Savannah, Georgia, where he borrowed a loaf of bread and woke up in jail.

Time now, my father is experimental animation: In moving black-and-white line drawings, a cat dreams a sphinx. A man with a briefcase gets tangled up in morning glory and reaches for a cloud. His hat becomes a cat, becomes a bird. The bird becomes the man's mind, and he meets a woman with fish eyes. The man passes a lake where a naked goddess bathes in sweet water. The man becomes the bird of his bird-mind and swings on the perch in his birdcage. His bird-mind has left his body; his body becomes a cat; the cat becomes a woman with bird-eyes. She picks an apple, follows the bird-body upstairs, and they chase each other and they make a mess of the soft-carpeted dining room and they fall asleep on the couch where the cat dreams of a sphinx. The sphinx plays like a kitten, unfurls a scroll that shows the man's bird-mind; she paws at it and he flies away. It's the sphinx who's been dreaming all this time.

My father says, "All of human history is the dream of the sphinx." And the two of us curl our bodies up tight and we squeeze ourselves hard until we become morning-glory seeds and we open the basement window and we let the wind carry us out onto the beach— we are seeds becoming.

My father says, "Morning glory is ambitious," and I'm back in my body with the seed in my chest and it sprouts and grows fast from me, vines out across the sand and through the stand of eucalyptus trees, and it creeps across the beach with its green arms and bright purple flowers. My father says, "Listen," and when I listen hard, I can hear the morning glory whispering, "Grow," and I can hear the trees promise to shelter us and my father says, "Listen," and the sand whispers, too, and the ocean in its vastness whispers, "Yes," and I stand on one leg and I hop like my grandpa but my father says, "Shhhh," and I stand perfectly still and watch as waves of light emanate from our bodies and the wind moves our energy and the ocean curls into waves and the waves crash on our shore and we become the ocean.

BOOK 4

Shame Theories

Brazen Hussy

I'd always been a slow reader, and plodding through the masculine mire of classical English slowed me down even more, but Lola and I signed up for the same nineteenth-century lit class and I still had that old copy of *The Scarlet Letter* my mother mailed me back in Rome, so nights after the kids fell asleep we lay on Lola's carpeted floor and we sipped black tea and we read to each other.

Picture the Puritan crowd in colonial Boston: "A throng of bearded men in sad-colored garments and gray steeple-crowned hats, intermixed with women, some wearing hoods, and others bareheaded . . ."

It's in front of all these scolds that Hester Prynne is marched out, holding her baby girl and wearing a beautifully embroidered red letter *A* for "adulterer." She's forced to stand for three hours in front of this crowd, exposing the marks of her sluttiness while they gasp and taunt and point. It was the original American campaign to prevent out-of-wedlock pregnancy, but even the townspeople in that scene know that something isn't right. The red letter Hester wears—meant to shame her into humiliation and self-disdain—doesn't seem to faze her all that much. Instead, "It had the effect of a spell, taking her out of the ordinary relations with humanity, and enclosing her in a sphere by herself."

Maybe when you live in a town full of drab gossips, a sphere by one's self isn't so bad. Maybe what shame requires to stay alive is the consent of the shamed.

"She hath good skill at her needle, that's certain," one female spectator notices, "but did ever a woman, before this brazen hussy, contrive such a way of showing it! Why, gossips, what is it but to laugh in the faces of our godly magistrates, and make a pride out of what they, worthy gentlemen, meant for a punishment?"

"I'll make pride out of punishment!" Lola laughed, and she finished off her tea and opened a bottle of wine.

Maybe the antidote to shame is to make pride out of punishment.

Here's *The Scarlet Letter*'s backstory: Hester comes to the new country from England alone, but already married. Her husband, an older scholar and doctor, arrives a few years later, having given Hester time to have a secret affair with the hot young pastor in town and get knocked up. When the old husband finally gets to Boston, it's on the very day of Hester's public shaming. He doesn't identify himself to the crowd and Hester doesn't out him. Only she knows her husband is there. And only she knows who Pearl's father is.

As the story deepens, Hester and Pearl, alienated from their community, go and live in a sweet little abandoned cottage on the outskirts of town where Hester takes care of Pearl and does needlepoint. Her work is all the rage in town—her walk of shame wasn't a bad advertisement for her skill—but she can't charge much. Being female as she is, and practicing the only art available to women, Hester barely ekes out a living as she makes those ruffled collars and armbands for the wealthy gentlemen of Boston.

When Hester finishes a fancy pair of gloves for the governor, she takes the opportunity to go and see him herself and try and have a word with him about keeping custody of Pearl. There's been talk around town that the child should be taken away from her and given to a nice Christian couple just like Rush Limbaugh still says on the AM radio to anyone who'll listen because he doesn't think hussies like us can raise politically docile children.

Pearl is three years old at this point—the same age as Maia now—and Hester dresses her in scarlet-red velvet.

The drab Puritan town kids harass the little family as they make their way toward Governor Bellingham's mansion, but Pearl is tough and scrappy and she fights those kids off and she and her mother get to the mansion just fine and the hot pastor happens to be there and Hester's old husband, too, and the pastor says a few words in Hester's defense so she can keep her baby.

For now, anyway, she can keep her baby.

But that husband who has dedicated himself to figuring out who Hester hooked up with—well, he puts it together, like, *ah-ha.*

As Hester and Pearl leave the governor's mansion, the governor's sister, Ann Hibbins, calls down to them from a window and invites Hester to a witches' sabbath in the woods. Hester tells the witch that she'd gladly go, but she has to keep custody of her little girl.

As an aside, it is historically true that Governor Bellingham of Massachusetts had a widowed sister named Ann Bellingham Hibbins. Prior to the Salem witch trials but after the years covered in *The Scarlet Letter*—between 1648 and 1656—five women were executed for witchcraft in Boston. The last one, unlike the first four, was wealthy and socially prominent: Anne Bellingham Hibbins. The minister John Horton later commented on her execution: "Mistress Hibbins was hanged for a witch only for having more wit than her neighbors." It's unclear whether Governor Bellingham was unable to save his sister or if he refused. His name is absent from the news articles of that time.

But back to fiction: Hester's husband rolls out his revenge. Picture him rubbing his little hands together. Yes, he'll befriend the young minister and, under the guise of moral and philosophical chitchat, he'll start tormenting the pastor until his guilt at having not only fathered Pearl but having let Hester take the fall alone haunts him like a thousand grisly phantoms—"in many shapes, of death, or more awful shame, all flocking round about the clergyman, and pointing with their fingers at his breast!"

In his torment, it's almost like the pastor learns a fraction of what it means to be female every day.

The more plagued the young clergyman feels, the more his Puritan community swoons for him: "The virgins of his church grew pale around him, victims of a passion so imbued with religious sentiment that they imagined it to be all religion, and brought it openly, in their white bosoms, as their most acceptable sacrifice before the altar . . ."

Meanwhile, Hester and Pearl live in sweeter and sweeter peace in her cottage by the sea: "The tendency of her fate and fortunes had been to set her free. The scarlet letter was her passport into regions where other women dared not tread. Shame, Despair, Solitude! These had been her teachers—stern and wild ones—and they had made her strong . . ."

Pearl, for her part, grows naughtier and witchier every year.

Hester's exes keep themselves mired ever deeper in the muck of their own guilt and vengeance. Finally, Hester sees that the whole thing has gone too far, and she tells her one-time lover that her husband's the one who's been messing with his head. The pastor is angry, of course—he'd thought it was his own conscience killing him—and he even blames Hester for not cluing him in earlier, but he's a forgiving kind of guy, this hot preacher, and he finally makes a great public spectacle of his confession and then drops dead for extra drama.

Hester's husband dies pretty soon himself, leaving a surprisingly large estate to the young and still-witchy Pearl. Now she's the richest heir in the New World and she and Hester take off for a few years on a well-deserved vacation, and eventually Pearl settles down—back in Europe, where they don't hang witches anymore, we hope—and Hester comes home to her sweet little cottage by the sea, and she's definitely a hag, and she lives happily there—and unmarried—forever after.

The End

Etymology

Bra • **zen:** *adj.* [Old English] Made of brass.
Hus • **sy:** *n.* [Late Middle English] Contraction of housewife.

Brass housewife.
Brazen hussy.

Insults Reserved for the Feminine Besides "Brazen Hussy"

Nasty

Bitch

Cunt

Slut

Whore

Puta

Tart

Bimbo

Floozy

Skank

Twat

Ho

Tramp

Trollop

Jezebel

Loose

Marimacha

Dyke

Clam bumper

Muff diver

Carpet muncher

Dick tease

Ballbuster

Hysterical

Hormonal

Bossy

Witch

Wench

Shrill

Bruja

Shrew

Abrasive

High-maintenance

JAP

Slag

Frigid

Frumpy

Sow

Cow

Daft cow

Heifer

Dragon lady

Dame

Broad

Harpy

Nag

Woosie

Ditz

Airhead

Bombshell

Faggot

Fag

Pansy

Sissy

Poof

Mangina

Nellie

Swish

Pussy

Tuna

Gash

Slit

Hole

Bridezilla

Gold digger

Welfare queen

Bad mother

Spinster

Old maid

Hag

I can only think of three or four insults reserved for the masculine.

Basically Poison

I needed $2,500 and fast if I was going to hire a family-law attorney to get me out of the mess my empowerment had gotten me into, and here on the back page of the *San Francisco Bay Guardian* was a bold-print ad:

OVUM DONORS NEEDED
$3,000 for your eggs. Healthy women aged 18–25 who
have already given birth successfully preferred.

I was *preferred*! My having given birth was described as *successful*! Yes, I had *successfully* given birth. I am *preferred*! I dialed the number and I buckled Maia into her car seat and we drove the half hour and through the tunnel to Walnut Creek and we found the office in the strip mall and we stepped inside and took in the walls decorated with hand-colored black-and-white photographs of white children.

The woman who interviewed me seemed surprised that I'd brought Maia.

It hadn't occurred to me not to bring Maia.

We were preferred! We were successful!

I breastfed her while I took the Minnesota Multiphasic Personality Inventory, and I let a nurse shoot me up with hormones she said would make me hyper-ovulate and might, I acknowledged in the written release, increase my risk for stroke, sudden death, and certain cancers, and had a 50 percent chance of rendering me infertile.

What did it matter? $3,000 was more money than I'd ever heard of receiving.

$2,500 for the family lawyer and what would we do with the other $500? Maybe I'd get glasses. I hadn't told anyone, but I'd been having trouble making out street signs since sophomore year.

I smiled wide, thinking about crisp vision.

The nurse looked down at her pink manicured nails and said, "According to your personality test, you tend to deny your anger." She shrugged like it didn't matter. "You can come back next month for the ovum harvest."

And I nodded, still smiling, "Okay!" even though I was starting to feel angry.

The nurse said, "Um, you'll have to stop breastfeeding your daughter now." The nurse didn't smile or frown when she said that. "Your milk is basically poison now. Because of the injections I gave you."

I stood there looking at the nurse, my eyes filling with tears. I knew child-led weaning was best, and it was the free food we'd relied on for almost four years now, but I knew, too, that I needed $2,500 and fast if I wanted to hire the lawyer to make sure Maia didn't go to foster care, so I squeezed her little hand and I whispered, "It's okay," and Maia squeezed my hand back, and I felt like such a sucker right then for falling for that dumb ad in the *San Francisco Bay Guardian*.

Of course no one thought I was preferred.

Of course no one thought I was successful.

That night I dreamed I gave birth to baby after baby and the wealthy, middle-aged married couples of Walnut Creek feasted on my children's flesh with sharp forks, leaving my cut body in its pool of blood and poison.

I didn't go back to that office decorated with hand-colored black-and-white photographs for the harvest.

There was nothing I could do now about my milk being poisoned, but fuck them.

They couldn't have my preferred and successful eggs.

I mean, seriously. Fuck them.

To Attract Urgent Money

You have to do this spell at a quarter to midnight.

Get one white votive candle for every $100 or $1,000 you need. (So, for example, if you need $300 or $3,000, that's three candles, etc.) Arrange them in a circle on a plate you actually use.

Sit in an otherwise dark room.

Light a gold or green candle to see by.

Visualize a circle of golden light around you for protection and a circle of blue light around that for healing.

Moving clockwise around your plate, pick up each unlit votive, light it from the main candle, and as you do, announce that the candle you're lighting represents the $100 or $1,000.

Set each lit candle back down in the circle.

When the whole circle is lit, say a prayer explaining that you're not greedy, but the money is necessary.

Let the candles burn out of their own accord, placing them somewhere very safe—even in the sink—if you have to leave them unattended.

Since the Baby

"Ms. Gore?" the psychologist leaned forward in her chair. "Ms. Gore, what is the court to make of your inability to maintain a serious relationship?"

"What?" I squeaked in a voice that felt weird to me. I had my hands folded in the lap of a borrowed floral skirt, and I had my legs crossed at the ankles and everything felt weird to me. I was this twisted version of myself, so maybe I shouldn't have been surprised when my voice came out sounding like I'd inhaled helium.

The psychologist said, "According to my notes, you haven't been in a serious relationship since the baby?"

Her notes?

Since the baby?

The skin of the psychologist's cleavage was freckled, and I thought that was kind of hot. I closed my eyes, trying to put that out of my mind. I mean, *What was wrong with me?* It hadn't occurred to me that I was supposed to be in a serious relationship since the baby. I was twenty-two years old and I hadn't had sex in more than a year. In Petaluma, I was *die welfare slut*, and here I was supposed to be in a serious relationship since the baby?

The psychologist tilted her head to the side. "Ms. Gore, are you bisexual?"

My throat constricted.

Was I?

Bisexual?

I looked out the window, and I let my gaze follow the branch of a gnarled Australian tea tree. *What would it mean to be bisexual? Would it mean I would lose my daughter or not lose my daughter? Would it mean they would cut my breasts with hot irons? Would it mean they'd cut my hands and my arms? Would it mean I'd have to stand up in front of all the town shrews wearing a scarlet letter? Would it mean we could live by ourselves in a little thatched cottage by the sea?*

Was I bisexual?

How would I know?

Behind the tea tree, a couple of middle-aged women played in a tire swing. When I squinted, I could see they were bell hooks and Adrienne Rich swinging around in that tire.

bell waved at me, and I started to smile in recognition.

I had the urge to tell the psychologist that I was half schizophrenic and perhaps therefore prone to hallucinations. Maybe I'd say, "I'm actually bi-*psycheal.* More than bisexual."

But Adrienne put her finger to her lips like, *Shhh.*

I thought of the woman in the purple leotard back at the botanica in San Francisco, who said, "To know, to will, to dare, to keep silent." I ran my fingers through my curls. "What?" I blurted to the psychologist. "Bisexual? No. I'm just focusing on school right now. Oh my god," I kind of giggled, "bisexual?"

*

Now, instead of Lance coming to my apartment and me calling the cops on him when he broke things, I filled Maia's pockets with sprigs of rosemary and lemon verbena and I dropped her off at Lance's employer's apartment and I drove home fast and I sat in my closet with the phone, waiting for the cops to call me:

Mrs. Gore, there's a man drunk in public with a child, and the child has your name and number on a metal safety bracelet around her small wrist.

Mrs. Gore, there's a man on a motorcycle with a child hanging on for dear life, and the child has your name and number on a metal safety bracelet around her small wrist.

Mrs. Gore, during the raid of an illegal warehouse dwelling we found a child, and the child has your name and number on a metal safety bracelet around her wrist.

Mrs. Gore, we've picked up a man on an existing warrant, and the child in his custody has your name and number on a metal safety bracelet around her small wrist.

"Yes, thank you, officer. I'll be right there."

Sigil Magick

From *Experimental Magick:*
The Secret Lives of Witches:

*To cast a spell with a sigil, write your desire as
though it is already your truth, such as*

"I am a millionaire."

*Take out all the vowels and double letters so that
you're left with the basics:*

MLNR

*Now write and rewrite those letters, simplifying
and stylizing them until they're unrecognizable
and seemingly meaningless.*

*Draw your final sigil on a small piece of paper
and destroy it in a memorable manner. Trust that
the universe has received your message and forget
about it.*

"Maia is safe."

MSF

Violent Language

At Mills College, I learned that even language could be violent.

The women in my sociology class said we shouldn't use the phrase "rule of thumb" because it referred to an old English law that allowed a man to beat his wife with a stick so long as it wasn't thicker than his thumb.

The women in the statistics class I taught for work-study said I shouldn't use the phrase "take a stab at it" when I wanted them to intuit an answer. *I mean, was I trying to normalize knife violence?*

The women in my communications class said we shouldn't refer to the dots on our lists as "bullet points."

I quite liked this strange new game.

I'd always been a slow talker because my own words echoed in my head and I wondered what they meant, so I appreciated this idea of everybody slowing down and considering their metaphors before they blurted whatever sprang to mind.

But I also wanted to sharpen my words into weapons.

I wanted to sit shotgun.

I wanted to take a stab at it.

Would we have a conflict here?

Would nonviolent language mean continuing to deny my anger?

On Sunday morning, I woke before dawn and carried Maia across the driveway to Lola's apartment.

The new baby's father, Piedro, watched all the kids.

Lola made our coffee.

I cut the cardboard stencils.

And the two of us headed downtown.

I could feel all my blood pulsing through all my veins as we tagged the county court buildings, gently, with red spray paint:

MISOGYNY: LOOK IT UP, STAMP IT OUT

The other women at Mills College would accuse us of perpetuating violent language with the "stamp it out" part of our graffiti—we knew that—but we wanted to perpetuate some violence.

Lola, it turned out, had only been fourteen years old when she got pregnant with Leena by an Oakland cop. When her mother complained to the courts about statutory rape, the judge ordered Lola to take her daughter to the cop's apartment in Hayward every Wednesday and Saturday evening.

Tagging that county court building with MISOGYNY: LOOK IT UP, STAMP IT OUT was the only violence left to us.

"Do you have a spirit guide?" Lola asked me, all earnest

as we headed home on the bus with our empty spray-paint cans and our stained red stencil.

Maybe I just needed a spirit guide.

But when I closed my eyes and tried to picture what a spirit guide might look like, I realized my world was full of them: Artemis, who showed up a day late in Italy; my mother's best friend, Roberta, who turned into a possum to scare me awake; the witch back in Sonoma County who'd canceled our appointment and met me in the depth of the tree; the singing woman who'd turned into a herring as she tried to teach me to use every scrap, to not waste anything, to remember self-preservation is sometimes more important than empowerment. The writers who spoke to me on their pages of their closet books and visited me in the twilights of my waking hours were spirit guides too. Weren't they?

*

My phone rang early. I picked it up, but it wasn't anyone calling from family court. It was an organizer from a famous national feminist organization—let's call it Famous National Feminist Organization. She'd gotten my number from my editor at *Sonoma County Women's Voices* and she wanted to know if I'd be up for a demonstration that weekend.

Of course.

They already had another woman who'd agreed to do it. The two of us would wear wedding dresses and we'd stand out on the steps of the Alameda County court building and we'd have a faux gay wedding. We'd be pronounced wife and wife and we'd kiss and the press would take pictures and we'd all have a grand time.

"All right," I agreed.

I mean, Why not?

Maia and Leena could be the flower girls.

I met the organizer from Famous National Feminist Organization at a coffee shop in Berkeley. She wore a purple sweater. She handed me a hundred dollars cash "for costuming." So I spent fifty dollars on an over-the-top satin wedding dress at the Goodwill on Broadway in downtown Oakland, the other fifty on groceries.

The next morning, when I put on the wedding dress, I was surprised that it made me immediately horny. I'd never consciously fantasized about weddings or marriage. Where had the association come from? This wedding dress = sex = hot? What kind of terrible rom-com movies had gotten into my head? The royal wedding of my childhood—Charles and Diana—was the only time besides *Roots* that we were allowed to watch TV.

Oh, who cared why?

I loved that hideous dress.

I never wanted to take it off.

I made myself a strong cup of coffee, poured Maia a bowl of Toasty O's.

Later, she'd stand by my side with a little bouquet of jasmine flowers she picked from the Mills College community garden.

The woman I married wasn't my type. She was wispy and straight, and she instinctively wiped her lips just after I'd kissed her.

Still, we were a pretty picture in the newspapers.

After our wedding ceremony was over and the press packed up their cameras and Maia and Leena played freeze tag on the cement expanse, a pretty butch woman in a tuxedo approached me. "You know," she said, "Famous National Feminist Organization wouldn't let me and my fiancée get married today." She motioned to a Latina woman wearing a leather jumpsuit. "They were totally femme-centric."

I thought about that.

There was an actual gay couple who wanted to get married.

I myself had vowed never to get married.

And I'd been hired as a stand-in with my fake wife because we were a prettier picture: two white women in virgin-white wedding dresses.

I covered my face with my hands.

The butch crossed her arms against her flat chest, righteous in her tuxedo and her lavender bow tie. And she was right. Of course she was right.

What the straight girl and I had been a part of was staged and silly.

I didn't know what to say.

I stood there, all inexplicably turned-on in my Goodwill satin wedding dress, my body hardwired by every media wedding fantasy I didn't even know I'd taken in.

My feet hurt.

The faint smell of jasmine.

"Honey," I finally said, then realized how condescending I must have sounded but didn't know how to fix it. *How could I explain that handing your family over to the mercy of the government was no happy ending? Was in fact a patriarchal, capitalist trap?* I pointed vaguely to the county building behind me, to family court. Our MISOGYNY: LOOK IT UP, STAMP IT OUT graffiti had been whitewashed again. I shook my head. "You don't really want access to that place."

*

The court-appointed psychologist inched her glasses down her nose under the harsh fluorescent lights. "Ms. Gore, I understand you were once married to a woman."

I hesitated, then covered my mouth with a neatly manicured hand. "Oh, no," I demurred. "That was just a demonstration for Famous National Feminist Organization."

"Oh," the psychologist smiled. "I'm sorry," she said, "I just had to ask, you know?"

I kept my lips closed when I smiled.

"I do love the work of Famous National Feminist Organization," the psychologist assured me.

"Oh, I do too," I said, and I kept smiling even though my brain was punching through the walls of my skull with all kinds of violent language.

Spell to Prevail in Family Court

You'll need to sweeten the judge to your position. (You may adjust or adapt this spell to sweeten anyone to you under any circumstances.)

Get a small jar of honey or syrup—a short jar with a flat metal lid.

Now take a small piece of paper and write the name of the judge or whomever you need to sweeten three times like a list:

Judge's Name
Judge's Name
Judge's Name

Turn your piece of paper ninety degrees sideways and write your own name three times across, so that your name crosses the judge's names, kind of like a tic-tac-toe grid.

Now write your specific wish in a circle around the names—write this as one continuous circle of script, without spaces between the words. Don't even lift your pen to dot your i's or cross your t's. Your specific wish here can be very simple, such as, *helpmehelpmykidshelpmehelpmykidshelpme* or *favormefavormefavorme*.

It's okay if you have to do a few drafts of this paper. You want it to be just right.

Once you've got it right, you can sprinkle a little court-case powder on your paper if you have any.

Now, fold the paper toward yourself—you're bringing the sweetness toward yourself.

Open your jar of honey and have a spoonful. As you savor it, say, "As this honey is sweet to me, so will Judge _____ be sweet to me and favor me."

Press your paper into your honey and close the jar tight.

Now rub a small orange or brown candle with court-case oil if you have it—otherwise a little coconut oil will do. Melt the candle to the top of the honey-jar lid with hot wax and let the candle burn all the way down. As you watch the flame, picture yourself calm, self-preserving, and factual.

Do this candle-burning step every Monday, Wednesday, and Friday for as long as your case goes on, and say, whenever you think of it, "As this honey is sweet to me, so will Judge _____ be sweet to me and favor me."

And again picture yourself calm, self-preserving, and factual.

Gender Trouble

Maia and I climbed the steps to our apartment after her day at the lab school, found a small purple envelope next to the frog statue on my front steps, and Maia said, "What dis?"

I shrugged.

Inside the envelope, a fat joint and a small amethyst crystal rubbed against a note from Lola that said, simply:

You got this, girl.

"What dis?" Maia asked again.

"Nothing, baby."

I made macaroni and cheese from a box in our little kitchen.

After Maia fell asleep, I smoked the whole joint and lay down on our mattress. I noticed our sheets had blue flowers on them. I stared up at the ceiling, thinking.

Was I or was I not some man's property?

My art history teacher lectured about the virgin/whore dichotomy, but it felt like more than that. If Hester and Lola and I didn't have authoritarian fathers, and we didn't have husbands, and we did have children—proof of our nonvirginity—that made us the *other* female: the adulterer, the degraded, the slut, the drunk girl, the stripper, the reject, the unwed mother. In other words, fair game. *Isn't it a shame?*

They could call us names and make us wear red letters and rape us and force us to parent with our rapists or take our children away altogether. They could cut our cunts with steel blades and poison our breast milk and buy and sell our eggs and we'd have to spend any money we got on lawyers defending us, begging, *Pretty please just let me keep my child.*

They could burn us alive and make a public spectacle of it.

They could decide who was white enough to marry another woman.

I wanted to be a man-hater, but it had rarely been my fathers or my grandfathers who shamed me. That emotional work belonged first to the women's sphere. I wanted to blame violence solely on men, but it hadn't been my fathers who couldn't control their rage. Domestic violence in our home belonged first to my mother's sphere. I wished, some days, that I hadn't been born a female, but I could see that Lance and my fathers and my grandfathers were sometimes just as fucked by their own gendered blueprints for self-destruction.

I wanted not to self-destruct.

I got up and set the amethyst Lola had given me on the altar with my candles and poems and other stones.

I intend not to self-destruct.

Pandemic

My phone rang in the dark.

"Hello?"

Jamie choked on her words.

I could picture the way the glow from the streetlight came in through the little window of her closet.

She'd finally broken up with her girlfriend—against the advice of the *I Ching*—and her girlfriend, as promised, had killed herself.

"Where did you go?" Jamie cried. "I thought you and the baby were here in the closet waiting for me."

Had she really thought that? Or was she speaking metaphorically?

"I'm in Oakland," I said, not wanting to sound square in my literalism but not sure, either, if Jamie was crazy confused.

She read to me from Kathy Acker, *Empire of the Senseless*: "One must learn how to suicide in this world, for that's all that's left us." She exhaled hard into the phone, which made me want a cigarette. She whispered, "Maybe my lover wants me to follow her in suicide?"

The moon outside my kitchen window at Mills College held its breath.

Her lover.

"Can I come over?" Jamie asked.

And I said, "Of course, baby," but then I felt self-conscious for calling her "baby."

Jamie wasn't my baby.

I wasn't her mother.

Was suicide really all that was left us?

I started to roll a cigarette, wondered how Jamie's girlfriend had died.

Did she jump from the Golden Gate Bridge?

No one ever jumped from the Bay Bridge.

Did she slit her wrists?

I never wanted to die when I crushed my cigarettes into the thin skin of my arms. I just wanted to live and feel things. I was afraid life was trying to teach me not to feel things.

Jamie answered my unasked question. She said, "These drug dealers raped her and then she took a giant speed ball and died." Jamie's voice was flat as she said the words. "The drug dealers took pictures of her unconscious body. They wrote *whore* and *bitch* across the xeroxed pictures. The pictures are on all the telephone poles and in the bus shelters. The telephone poles and the bus shelters are everywhere."

I remembered the posters of the teen moms: DIRTY, REJECT, LOSER.

I could feel Jamie's story like crushed glass on my skin, see the telephone poles like a terrible urban forest, and I wanted not to believe her. It seemed like there were a lot of drugs in Jamie's world and I wondered if we didn't speak the same psychic language anymore. The people on the AM radio always said teen pregnancy ruined girls' lives, but my life with Maia seemed safe and warm and Jamie's seemed violent. I thought about the trouble I might already be in for not being married and for wanting to identify as a mother who had custody of her daughter, and I worried that Jamie might bring her violence into my world, so I said, "You know? Maybe I should just come over to your place?"

Was I treating Jamie like a pariah because she'd been a victim, or was this self-preservation?

I didn't know.

"The telephone poles are everywhere," she whispered.

As I hung up, I wondered if Jamie's girlfriend could feel shame anymore.

*

In our bedroom, I knelt and lifted the weight of Maia's toddler body from the mattress. "I'm sorry," I whispered to her as I carried her across the driveway to Lola's place, but I wasn't sorry about taking her to Lola's place. Maia would wake up happy with the kids and they'd dance to Joan Armatrading and they'd eat Toasty O's. The sorry I felt was more existential. Even if I didn't have words like *pandemic*, I'd known the world was terrible even before I'd decided to keep the baby. I'd knowingly ushered a child into a world where men plastered xeroxed pictures of us on telephone poles in hopes of sexually humiliating us before we died.

*

That night, Jamie and I lay on our bellies on the hardwood floor of her empty apartment as her roommate tattooed snakes down the flesh and bones of our spines.

Jamie's skin gleamed blue under the light bulb.

"You have to know this wasn't your fault," the roommate kept saying as she inked Jamie's flesh and wiped away the blood.

"It's undeniably my fault," Jamie said into the floorboards.

And of course it wasn't Jamie's fault.

Except in the way that it was.

"Take off the rest of your clothes," Jamie said to me as soon as her roommate had packed up her tattoo gun and slipped out the front door.

An L7 album played loud from another apartment in the building.

I unbuttoned my jeans, slipped them off. My skin tingled self-conscious as I stood there naked in the blue light, but I wanted Jamie to feel in control of something and I didn't mind if that something was me. I took a cigarette from the pack on the windowsill and lit it.

Jamie peeled off her clothes, too, so I was less alone in my exposure.

I scooted the pack of cigarettes toward her along the windowsill, crouched down against a wall.

The moonlight made everything glow strangely noir:

two naked girls sitting across from each other on hard wood. It was our life and it was our small attempt at making our lives into a story with vivid black-and-white scenes you could already almost picture at a film festival.

Jamie pushed her copy of *Empire of the Senseless* across the floor toward me and I reached for it.

She said, "Open to a random page, point to a random line, and read it. That will be the oracle that tells me if she wants me to suicide."

I took a long drag from my cigarette, opened the book, and read the line to myself: *I needed her in order to live.* I flipped to another page fast, read aloud, "I quickly chose a raped body over a mutilated or dead one." I ashed the cigarette onto the floor, took another drag.

"What does it mean?" Jamie whispered.

I closed the book. "It means you have to live, even if you're fucked up."

Jamie grinned at that. She started to laugh a sad laugh. "I can't believe my girlfriend fucking killed herself."

*

I first met Jamie when we were both seventeen and so high on ecstasy that even the walls and the floor pulsed with life, and I think Suzanne Vega was playing, and now I remembered that sad laugh from that first night.

What had we talked about?

I'd come home to the Bay Area after some travels

and planned to leave again as soon as I could get the money together for a ticket.

A few years later, Jamie showed me a story she'd worked on in her writing group about that night, and immediately her story eclipsed my actual memory of meeting her. My name in her story was Fiona. She'd written her story as fiction. But now her fiction had become my history. Fiona and a Jamie-like girl high on ecstasy meet at a party in San Francisco as the walls pulse and the floor pulses and they talk and talk and they walk outside and as the sun comes up they're making out under a mural on the corner of Capp Street and something.

Had Suzanne Vega played that night or only in Jamie's story of it?

I remembered the witch back in Sonoma County and the way she'd said, "If you don't like the fairy tales you've been handed, you don't have to conform to them. You can reauthor them. You can write your story however you choose." And now I understood what she meant in a shifting way.

I think about how "Ariel" in this story hardly ever has any agency over anything in her life, and how "Ariel Gore," the author, can write it any goddamn way she chooses.

Once upon a time, we projected our stories into each other's closets, and we bent and tattooed the spines of our own books, looking in, and we replaced our memories with the stories we made from them.

Jamie said, "Is it weird that we just got matching snake tattoos?"

I chewed my lip. "Probably weird on a lot of levels."

*

Outside, the telephone poles were everywhere.
Bitch.
Whore.

Outside, the bus shelters were everywhere.
Loser.
Reject.

Outside, the baby dolls were crucified red onto doors.
Die
Welfare
Slut.

Outside, the streetlights had already flickered on. *And you're going to get slapped across the face in front of whoever has come to dinner.*

Inside, we smoked naked under the blue light bulb trying hard to turn it all into art.

Once upon a time.

Decompensating

The less I slept, the less sleep I needed. *I bet geniuses don't need any sleep at all!* I would sleep just one hour each night. I wasn't a genius, but I could push myself toward it. I could live on cigarettes alone! I went to classes in the daytime, took care of Maia, and worked through the nights on the prototype for a zine called *Hip Mama* I intended to start as my senior project. My idea was to have a media that celebrated the shamed feminine. The woman at Marcus Books on MLK and the womyn at Mama Bears on Telegraph had both offered to sell the zine if I would make it.

Maia wore the same dirty overalls day after day.

We both brushed our teeth each morning at eight. *Someone unfit to mother would not keep such bright teeth.*

I started wearing the white satin wedding dress from the marriage protest all over town. I didn't have any shoes that looked right with it, so I went barefoot. I kept my toenails painted red. I felt turned-on all the time. I slept in heavy blue-and-black eye makeup and didn't wash my face. I liked the way that people either got romantically excited to see me in that dress or seemed genuinely concerned.

The baristas at Peet's gave me free coffee.

The Oakland cops followed me slowly in their patrol cars.

Lola had finally declared her major in psychology, and she said I was decompensating. I wore red lipstick, and she sighed and opened a bottle of Sierra Nevada Pale Ale. "Seriously, Ariel," she said, "there's a *DSM* code for this. You're falling apart."

Was I falling apart?

Mary TallMountain whispered to me from the altar: *You're this close to graduation, Ariel.*

I hated the way that I could be right here on the brink of a Freytag-overcoming/happy-culminating moment and then lose my shit again.

Why couldn't I ever have rising action?

I drank coffee. I thought of Rapunzel's haircut, and Augustine Gleizes. That's how they escaped. In Lola's bathroom, I shaved my head and watched the curls fall onto her linoleum floor.

Maia and Lyle played with her old Speak & Spell and they laughed.

"Spell *ocean*."

"R. H. T."

"That is incorrect."

I left them with Lola and walked down to my economics professor's office to hand in my invoice for work-study.

My professor squinted up at me from her desk. She didn't say anything about my white satin wedding dress. She just said, "Your hair?"

I fixed my gaze down at my muddy bare feet as I

handed over the time sheet. *You're this close, Ariel. Don't come undone now.* "I've been feeling out of control," I admitted.

And my economics professor nodded up at me, matter-of-fact, but loving, too, and she said, "Well. Now you have control of your hair."

Bodies of Resistance

My paper on shame was due on Friday, so I fastened Maia into her car seat and we drove down the 880 through all the suburban sprawl and we crossed the Dumbarton Bridge where the bay smells like salt and chickenshit and we eased through Whiskey Gulch and through the class-stratified neighborhoods of my childhood and we parked in front of the old elm-shaded Spanish house my stepdad's father built and I knocked on the giant door and here's my stepdad, John, all toothy jack-o'-lantern grin and wispy gray hair and he winked at me and said, "Well, hello, chick-a-dee," and he scooped Maia up in his strong arms and he said, "I have chocolate toffee in my desk."

Maia cackled. "Did fairies make your candy?"

But my stepdad looked confused by that question because he'd never been one for magical realism. "Well, I don't know about that," he said. "I suspect it was made in a factory."

No matter.

At the picnic table in my parents' patio, the three of us ate roasted beets and brown rice for dinner, ate chocolate toffee for dessert, and I asked John what he knew about shame.

My stepdad had been a Catholic priest for thirty

years before he met my mom. The Saturday after I finished kindergarten, I carried the flowers down the aisle at Stanford Memorial Church for their wedding. The letter from the archbishop arrived that afternoon: my stepdad had been excommunicated from the Catholic Church. Now he worked for minimum wage at Printer's Ink Bookstore.

He nodded. "Well, the Catholic Church has used shame in a number of ways over the centuries. They've used it to subjugate women, certainly, and a primary motivation for the subjugation of women is to keep property rights from them, of course, and equally because female sexuality terrified them. Greed and fear of 'the other' is always a dangerous combination." He smacked his lips, purple from the beets. He said, "The Church used shame more widely, too, as a tool to demoralize whole cultures for the sake of colonization." He shrugged, serious but resigned to it, too. "If a people are proud, they'll fight for their land rights. If a people feel ashamed, it's simply much easier to rob them blind."

What he said made sense.

He straightened his spine. "Of course they shamed me to the point of excommunication because I didn't do the usual thing and lie about having fallen in love. That's the reason most of the Catholic kids weren't allowed to play with you." He cleared his throat. "But of course the Catholic rule that barred priests from marrying had a lot more to do with inheritance laws and Church property than with sexual conservatism. Very few people in power really care about other people's sexuality. They care about money. But shaming sexuality is easier because that realm is so vulnerable. And of course if you control sexuality, that's power that can be transmuted into more money."

I'd always liked my stepdad.

Maia sucked on the chocolate toffee and she whispered to John, "I really think fairies made it."

*

Shame Theory
Ariel Gore
Independent Study 195: Feminist Economics and English Literature

White women and men of color earn approximately seventy-five cents for every dollar white men earn doing the same work. Women of color earn less than that.

That's the wage gap.

Women's fashion magazines cause 70 percent of us to feel depressed, guilty, and ashamed within just a few pages.

That's media, advertising, and the body police.

The faces of young mothers are plastered around the city with red words like "loser" and "reject" written across our chests.

That's the campaign to prevent teen pregnancy.

Nathaniel Hawthorne's 1850 novel, *The Scarlet Letter*, opens with the unwed mother Hester Prynne emerging from prison to her meet punishment in Puritan New

England. Supposedly in "great mercy and tenderness of heart," a panel of judges have spared Hester the death penalty. Instead, she will stand before the people of her community, who call her a brazen hussy, and she'll wear the red letter *A* for "adulterer" on her chest for the rest of her life.

In his 1975 essay "The Body of the Condemned," Michel Foucault notes that in capitalist society, to be "useful" to the economy, a body must be subjugated.

Considered another way: the untortured, unshamed body is of little use to capitalism.

If my body is never threatened or shamed, it will be difficult to get me to work for subpoverty wages. It will be difficult to get me to sign over my property. It will be difficult to get me to put your family before my own.

What does shame require to stay alive?
What is the antidote to shame?
What is my value as a subjugated body?
What might my value be as an empowered body?
What do I value?

Water carried through pipes has an economic value. Water carried for miles by women has no economic value. Economic valuation systems, accord to Marilyn Waring, author of *If Women Counted*, were originally developed to justify paying for war.

War can only appear to be profitable if women and children and poor people are worthless.

When I sell my eggs via a fertility clinic to a fortysomething married woman in Walnut Creek so that she and her husband can have a baby, my eggs have an economic value.

When I have a baby of my own, neither my eggs nor my baby has an economic value. If I have to buy infant formula, that has economic value. My breast milk has no value. If I'm an unmarried woman—a woman who has rejected the enslavement of my household labor—I become a threat to the entire system of economic valuation and, by extension, a threat to justifications for war. My likeness is then plastered in bus shelters all over the city and emblazoned with red words like "reject" and "dirty" and "loser." Like Hester Prynne's moment in *The Scarlet Letter*, my public shaming is not merely designed for my own benefit, but rather serves as a sermon and a warning to other girls and other women who may hope to escape the confines of a system designed to support and enable the white-supremacist capitalist war machine.

I reject this system.
I intend to resist this system.

The Woman from Spelman

I'd said "hi" to the woman from Spelman a couple of times since she moved into the apartment upstairs from ours—she was cute in a boyish kind of a way—but it still surprised me when I heard the knock on my door and opened it to find her standing there.

She was visiting for the semester, the woman from Spelman.

Bright brochures in the dean's office called our colleges "sister schools"—I guess because Mills and Spelman both started out as seminaries, both morphed into finishing schools, and both were now places where girls became womyn and practiced witchcraft and came out as lesbians.

"Sorry to bug you," the woman from Spelman said, and she held up a six-pack of Olympia. "I'm Athena, and um, I noticed you left your daughter with Lola and her kids and, um, I don't know if you drink beer or anything, but . . ."

I needed to finish the prototype for *Hip Mama*. But a beer with the cute woman from Spelman sounded altogether better, so I said, "Sure. C'mon in."

"What's up with the frog statue?" she asked, pointing down.

I blushed, shrugged. "It makes me feel like a grown-up."

Inside my apartment, Luna rubbed up against Athena's leg.

Athena pawed through my music, nervous.

I opened a beer for her and one for me.

She said, "Can we listen to Me'Shell NdegéOcello?"

And I said, "Sure."

So Athena slipped *Plantation Lullabies* into the tape player, and she sat down with me in the kitchen nook at my cigarette-burned table. "How do people even meet people at this school?"

How did people meet people other places?

I didn't know. "I mostly just scan my surroundings, looking for friendly resistance."

Athena smiled at that and sipped her beer. "I'm actually supposed to be working on a sculpture project that brings mythology and consent together tonight," she sighed. "It's not as easy as it sounds."

I didn't think it sounded easy. It was a popular assignment at Mills: take two disparate realms and coexist them—like a river and capitalism, like art and motherhood, like me and Athena. I was trying to combine economics and feminist journalism, myself, and having a helluva time of it.

Athena said, "I have to find an interesting intersection between mythology and consent."

I knocked back the rest of my beer and felt less shy than usual. I told Athena about the fairy tales—Rapunzel and Sleeping Beauty and the rest of them—and about the way they seemed to be grooming children for sexual assault.

Athena frowned. "I never thought of it that way." She sipped her beer. "Did you hear about those rules they made at Antioch College? Where you have to get consent for every little thing? Like, *Can I kiss you?*"

I actually knew a lot about that Antioch policy. I told Athena about my beautiful and excellent friend from high school who went to Antioch all hopeful and trying to do what they told us to do—*don't get pregnant, finish high school, go to college*—but her first date at Antioch was date rape and my friend knew she'd drop out, but she fought hard to get that consent policy in place before she left because *who are we if we're not allowed say no?* But now Antioch was the laughingstock of the AM radio, and the talk-show hosts said that Antioch's consent rules would mean the death of romantic spontaneity.

As if rape were romantic.

As if rape were spontaneous.

Athena nodded at my story. "Oh, wow."

"I actually have a copy of the policy," I piped up. I had it folded up in "Song of Myself," where I turned for grounding, so I brought it to the table and I read it out loud:

> Consent is defined as the act of willingly and verbally agreeing to engage in specific sexual conduct. The following are clarifying points:
> - Consent is required each and every time there is sexual activity.
> - All parties must have a clear and accurate understanding of the sexual activity.

- The person(s) who initiate(s) the sexual activity is responsible for asking for consent.
- The person(s) who are asked are responsible for verbally responding.
- Each new level of sexual activity requires consent.
- Use of agreed-upon forms of communication such as gestures or safe words is acceptable but must be discussed and verbally agreed to by all parties before sexual activity occurs.
- Consent is required regardless of the parties' relationship, prior sexual history, or current activity (e.g., grinding on the dance floor is not consent for further sexual activity).
- At any and all times when consent is withdrawn or not verbally agreed to, the sexual activity must stop immediately.
- Silence is not consent.
- Body movements and nonverbal responses such as moans are not consent.
- A person cannot give consent while sleeping . . .

"Can I kiss you?" Athena interrupted.

And I nodded fast. "Yes, you have to ask permission for each thing."

"What I meant," Athena kind of stuttered, "was, like, actually, *can I kiss you?*"

Oh. I felt surprised and embarrassed that I hadn't understood. I blushed, then laughed.

"It's okay," Athena said. "I'm not trying to be aggressive."

"No, no." I felt panicky that I'd missed my opportunity to consent. "I mean, yes," I said. "We can kiss."

Me'Shell NdegéOcello sang from the cassette player about the colonized mind and loving oneself.

"I would like to consent," I said again, and I felt like such a nerd right then, but I liked it.

"Wow," Athena said. "All right." Her lips felt soft against mine. She whispered, "May I place my hand on your waist?"

"Yes?" I felt embarrassed that my ribs stuck out like I didn't eat, but I liked Athena's hand on my skin.

She whispered, "Do you wanna have a safe word that means no or do you wanna just keep asking for yes?"

I said, "Keep asking for yes." Something in the asking turned me on.

Athena's skin smelled like sandalwood.

"I think it's hot," I whispered. So many times I'd felt sexually shy because I always got nervous—Like, *what if my lover didn't like something I did?* Now I felt emboldened—Like, *I could really just ask?* So I whispered what I wanted in Athena's ear, and the moon outside my apartment felt happy.

What is the value of a soft, consensual kiss?

"con" means "with"
"consensual" means "with sensual."
What is the value of the moonlight?

The moon liked this Mills College just fine.

Athena breathed into the moonlight, and she said, "Oh my god, yes please."

Since September

I sent Mary TallMountain an invitation to my graduation, but it came back in a white envelope with an unfamiliar San Francisco return address and a note that read,

Dearest Ariel,

I am so sorry to have to inform you, but Mary died in September. Know that she always spoke warmly of you and your daughter, and she took great pride in the article you wrote about her for Sonoma County Women's Voices.

Congratulations on your graduation.

Sincerely,

Karen

How could it have been that I hadn't called Mary TallMountain since September? I started crying and couldn't stop. *Wasn't Mary supposed to be always dying and always keeping on? How could she die? What was the point in going to college and graduating if it meant you didn't call your friend since September— didn't even realize you hadn't called your friend since September?*

Luna jumped up onto the altar and I looked at Mary's poem. *Push through, Ariel. Just graduate. Even if it's pointless.*

Convocation

They called our graduation from Mills College a "convocation."
"Con" means "with."
"Convocation" means "with vocation"—like "with job."

Congratulations on your *with job*!
So much less shameful than *with child.*
*How much money do you owe the capitalist government
now that you're qualified to be an employee?*
Shut up, voices in my head.
Only crazy people talk to themselves, Ariel.

*

I ironed my black gown for my convocation and as I moved the iron back and forth across the towel on the table, I recited the beginning of that Tillie Olson story in *Tell Me a Riddle*: "I stand here ironing, and what you asked me moves tormented back and forth with the iron."

I breathed in, breathed out, like I was Tillie Olsen's character myself right then. And that's when I noticed the woman sitting on the other side of the table. She had curly gray hair and a closed-mouth smile.

In the story, it's a teacher or a social worker who has come to Tillie Olsen's character, saying, "I wish you would manage the time to come in and talk with me about your daughter. I'm sure you can help me understand her. She's a youngster who needs help and whom I'm deeply interested in helping."

Tillie Olsen's character had tried to follow all the good-mother rules in all the good-mother books of the 1950s, but she had to work too, of course, as a single mom. Her daughter was always good, and Tillie Olsen's character wonders now, "What in me demanded that goodness in her? And what was the cost, the cost to her of such goodness?"

Maia pulled at my graduation gown on the table but knew not to touch the iron. Maia had always been good—*poised*, her preschool teacher had said—and I wondered if that goodness had come at a terrible cost to her. Did I demand that goodness in her?

I looked at the woman across the table, and I said, "Tillie, what am I going to do after this?"

She nodded, still grinning, and she said, "You're going to keep trying not to divide yourself up into separate selves. Keep integrating everything."

To graduation, I carried Maia on my hip. Her four-year-old body felt heavy on mine, but everything in this stance represented "college" to me. I said, "Baby, we did it."

Under a clear blue sky on the green expanse of Mills College, my mother and stepdad sat on folding chairs.

My parents. I had expected them both.

My mother wore black.

As I hugged her thin frame, I tried to psychically communicate to her that I understood she was an artist who became a mother pre–*Roe v. Wade* in a culture that never said she could be both, and in a place where hardly anyone ever said, "Do whatever you want."

My stepdad wore a red beret.

The person I didn't expect to see on that green expanse was my real father—standing tall and bald in a Hawaiian shirt and suit pants—I didn't even know what to call him in the context of my larger family. My "real" father? My "biological" father? Both those sounded strange and dismissive. He was my father. In the basement apartment of my grandparent's house on Carmel Beach, he'd always just been my father. But I'd never seen him in the same space as my mother before. Would it be disloyal to her to acknowledge him? I tried to adjust. *Like, whatever.*

I put Maia down and she ran to Gammie Evelyn. Safety smelled like Paloma Picasso perfume.

I dug my fingernails into my wrists.

Athena smoked on a low concrete wall far away and I tried to signal to her that I needed a cigarette by tapping two fingers to my lips, but she didn't seem to read me.

My real father nodded at my mother and he laughed and said, "You look like a senior citizen," and she laughed at that, too, and I made a point of remembering it because it would be the only sentence I ever heard my parents exchange, but then my muscles felt hard against my bones as it occurred to me that my mother and my father knew each other.

I mean, of course my parents knew each other—but I'd never thought about it before. They'd been a couple once. *I mean, how random.*

And now my father pulled a video camera out of his bag, and he trained his lens on the tits and asses of the all the hot Mills girls around me, and in his movie version of the day, I do not exist.

Off camera, Athena brought me a cigarette.

Thank god she brought me a cigarette.

When I got back to my relatives, smelling like nicotine and still sporting the shaved head no one had commented on, my Gammie Gore stood next to my father in her tweed suit, and it occurred to me that her presence—more than anyone else's—meant that I'd maybe done something important.

My Gammie Gore never graduated from college. She went to art school in New York City in the 1930s, but when she announced her plan to move in with her female "best friend," her father insisted she come home and get married.

No "come home and get married" = no my father.

Isn't that right?

No my father = no me.

Come home, get married, get pregnant, slap the baby, and see if he cries alive.

If my Gammie Gore had stayed in art school in New York City in the 1930s, no me—and no need for me.

I thought about that.

Sixty years of evolution wasted on resistance to female education and cohabitation!

My father never finished college either.

He'd been happy studying architecture at UC Berkeley, reading E. E. Cummings and Allen Ginsburg in café basements, and going into the jazz clubs in the city, but he refused to go to ROTC and refused to register for the draft and that was that.

No war machine cooperation = no college for you.

I gave my father a quick hug and then turned and opened my arms toward my Gammie Gore, and I said, "Oh my god, you came to my graduation!" and my Gammie Gore kind of stepped back, like she didn't know whether to think I was too weird to acknowledge as a granddaughter or the only person who'd ever loved her even close to unconditionally.

My Gammie Evelyn approached us now too. She wore black-and-red silk, and she extended her hand to my Gammie Gore, and she said, "Well, hello, Ginny," and my Gammie Gore smiled back at my Gammie Evelyn and she said, "Well, hello, Evelyn," and my muscles began to soften against my bones as I took in the fact that my Gammie Gore and my Gammie Evelyn knew each other.

I mean, if my parents had once been a couple it only made sense that their mothers knew each other. All these separate family members I'd only known in separate spheres had pasts with each other and relationships I knew nothing about. I felt overwhelmed. I thought maybe we'd all go out to Home of Chicken and Waffles after this convocation, and then I'd begin to piece it all together. But none of my relatives invited me to Home of Chicken and Waffles or anyplace else after the ceremony; they just gave me quick hugs, one by one, and they wandered off toward the parking lot. At first I felt funny about that, like, *How rude of them.* But as a few wispy clouds gathered in the sky above Mills College and those clouds turned into witches' pillows and Maia pointed at the sky and said, "See the fairy wings?" and butterflies danced in the sunlight, I decided to reverse the meaning of my relatives' rudeness: truly, each of them had gotten out of bed that morning dreading who they might run into at my graduation—who they hadn't seen in twenty-three years—and they'd shown up anyway.

And one explanation for that showing up could be interpreted as love.

I decided that each of my relatives felt just alienated enough from the whole that they assumed I already had plans with the others and they didn't want to embarrass themselves by intruding and potentially flagging themselves as the sole pariah.

Shame = embarrassment.
Shame = estrangement.
Shame can look a lot like rude.

It's basically poison.

I slung my ironed black graduation gown over my shoulder and I took Maia's hand and we trudged back up the hill to our on-campus apartment and this whole graduation thing felt pretty anticlimactic. "Closer to Fine" blared from a car stereo, and one of my fellow graduates screamed along to that part about spending four years prostrate to the higher mind, getting her paper, and being free.

I scanned the trees for our red-winged blackbird, but saw no one.

I thought my degree would feel like freedom—like my road out of poverty—but all it meant now was that we had to move out of our on-campus apartment by Saturday.

I couldn't imagine how I might look for a job or begin to make a living except by buying books at garage sales like I'd always done and reselling them to used book dealers who ran their businesses out of VW vans like I'd always done and lighting candles on moonlit windowsills and hoping for the best.

Maia said, "Look!" and she pointed at the ground, and she squatted to pick up a little clear-quartz crystal, and as she handed it to me, she said, "Fairies made it."

"Congratulations, girl!" Lola called to us from across the driveway. "Do you wanna come out to Olive Garden with all of us and my dad?"

But I didn't know what Olive Garden was and I didn't have any money so I just called back, "Congratulations to you, too, girl! We already have plans!"

Inside our apartment, Maia played with her witch doll and pretended our couch was a tower and the witch was Rapunzel and she rescued herself. Maia had it all mixed up.

I changed into my REJECT T-shirt and jeans, put a cup of rice in the steamer, opened a can of black beans, and went to cut a sweet onion before I realized it was rotten.

A hard knock at the door, and I answered it. A woman in a purple blouse handed me a business card. "Child Protective Services," she said. "I need to come inside."

I could feel all the blood in my body flowing upward, fast and afraid.

I said, "Of course. Come in."

Was I allowed to not let her in?

Maia smiled at her and pursed her lips. "Are you a witch?"

"We're reading Rapunzel," I explained to the social worker as she sniffed around the corners of my house.

"The complaint says your house is filthy, but it looks fine."

I'd cleaned up in case my Gammie Evelyn had wanted to stop by.

The social worker took off her glasses. "The complaint says you wear a wedding dress every day?"

I shook my head fast. "That was performance art. For Famous National Feminist Organization."

"Oh," the social worker chirped.

Was it illegal to wear a wedding dress every day?

"Who made the complaint?"

The social worker looked at her clipboard and shook her head. "That's confidential." She looked out my window and squinted. "It's usually an ex."

"Lance or Jamie?"

But the social worker just shook her head. "That's confidential."

I felt so angry right then I wanted to cry, but instead I looked up at my altar, and I thought of all the living and dead writers, and I breathed in. *I am a mother who has custody of her child.* I would be calm and factual.

The social worker scanned the apartment again and said, "Well, I'm going to mark this complaint as unsubstantiated, but if we get another complaint we'll have to open an investigation."

"Thank you," I said, and I swallowed hard. I would have to be more careful.

A soft knock at the door, and I answered it, and here was Athena in baggy jeans and a T-shirt.

"Hey," I whispered, and I scanned the area to make sure the social worker was gone.

Athena smiled awkward. "Congratulations, girl," and she held out a book—*Written on the Body* by Jeanette Winterson—"I brought you a present."

And I felt happy.

I still had a couple beers from the six-pack she'd brought the other day, and I offered her one, opened one for myself, and I poured Maia a glass of the goat's milk she drank now that my milk was poison, and we all sat around our cigarette-burned table drinking goat's milk and beer and eating rice and beans.

I said, "Did you finish your sculpture and mythology project?"

And Athena gestured out my window and we all looked up to the giant clay-and-felt frog that suddenly loomed over our on-campus apartment building.

Maia gasped. "A magic frog?"

I couldn't believe I hadn't noticed it before. "What does it mean?"

Athena scooped a spoonful of rice and beans into her mouth and chewed and grinned. "Well, the frog's symbolic meanings are all about cleansing, renewal, fertility, abundance, and metamorphosis. But then I thought about what you were saying about fairy tales the other day, and I thought about the princes who get turned into frogs in the fairy tales, and I thought maybe that wasn't punishment, necessarily, you know? My hypothesis is that the frog actually represents consent. The frog represents the prince after his sight has been restored and he's free of the world of blind male entitlement. The frog is masculinity without the socialization of entitlement. Once the prince gets it—gets that he should knock if he wants to come in—he can stay a frog or turn back into a prince. Either way, it doesn't matter. The frog represents consent, and what it means to dig consent. What do you think?"

What did I think? I thought Athena was beautiful. I thought her hypothesis was kind of a stretch, but I lifted my beer can in a toast and said, "I think it's a worthy hypothesis."

That night, Athena and I slept under thrift-store blankets in my living room and Maia slept on our mattress in the bedroom and candles flickered on our windowsills for urgent money and my eyelids felt heavy like relief.

In the faint blue light of sunrise, the giant frog statue outside winked at me.

Athena slept.

Maia called from our bedroom. "Mama? Mama read?"

So I crept in and curled up next to her, and I whisper-read from Gloria Anzaldúa: "We preserve ourselves through metaphor; through metaphor we protect ourselves. The resistance to change in a person is in direct proportion to the number of dead metaphors that person carries. But we can also change ourselves through metaphor. And, most importantly, we can share ourselves through metaphor—attempt to put, in words, the flow of some of our internal pictures, sounds, sensations, and feelings and hope that as the reader reads the pages these 'metaphors' will be 'activated' and live in her."

"Met-phors," Maia whispered.

These metaphors are activated and live in you.

Just Because It's a Magic Apple Doesn't Mean There Isn't a Worm in It

Student Loan Account Statement
September 1, 2017

US Department of Education
Ariel Gore

Account Number: XXXXXXX1970
Current Balance: $127,862
Original Loan Amount: $32,000
Interest Rate: 8.25%
Status: Repayment
Current Monthly Payment: $1,255.70

Why They're Called Spells

I'm riding shotgun in the car, Maia at the wheel. My nine-year-old son, Max, calls out random math calculations from the back seat. It's twenty-three years later, so you know we survived. It turns out we can overcome without Freytag's pyramid—it just feels different than what we expected. As we pass Mills College, I point and say, "Maia and I used to live there—when she was small!" And I count back the years. "That was half my life ago."

And Max squeals, "*Ah!*" because he likes numbers and symmetry, and he looks out his window and through that fence into all those old eucalyptus trees, and he says, "It looks magical in there."

And Maia smiles her witchy smile. "It's true—there were fairies at Mills College."

And Max says, "*Oooh.*"

And we keep driving.

We drive through days and nights, through cities and cornfields, past strip malls and shuttered libraries, through forests and deserts. We're cutting a line through the heart of America.

We're trying not to live shitty lives.

We grew strong.

We grew bound up with amazement.

We are brazen hussies.

We transmute shame into power.

We care for children and elders.

We are evolution delayed by resistance.

When our mothers couldn't name us, we named ourselves.

We do whatever we want.

Some months we don't know how we'll manage the rent.

Let alone our student loan payments.

We're still clawing the fuck out of this hole we didn't dig.

We light candles for urgent money.

We still struggle with addictions.

But we've made a pact not to groom each other for the Brothers Grimm.

We make spells out of words.

W-R-D.

That's why they're called spells.

As we drive, I read aloud from "I Stand Here Ironing" by Tillie Olsen like it's some kind of mantra, like it could be our new ancestor: "Only help her to know— help make it so that there is cause for her to know— that she is more than this dress on the ironing board, helpless before the iron."

We are indebted.

We keep driving. We're headed east to see Hester Prynne in her cottage by the sea. She's an old hag by now and we're pilgrims and I think, *I want that.*

Cancel, cancel—*I intend that.* A cottage by the sea where I can definitely be a hag: *The scarlet letter was her passport into regions where other women dared not tread. Shame, Despair, Solitude! These had been her teachers—stern and wild ones—and they had made her strong.*

I loved my stern and wild teachers. They said, *If you don't like the fairy tales you've been handed, Ariel, you don't have to conform to them. You can reauthor them. You can write your story however you choose.*

The End

Reading List

Ariel by Sylvia Plath

"Song of Myself" by Walt Whitman

The Heart of a Woman by Maya Angelou

for colored girls who have considered suicide/when the rainbow is enuf by Ntozake Shange

Jambalaya by Luisah Teish

The Book of Sand by Jorge Luis Borges

Silences by Tillie Olsen

Sister Outsider by Audre Lorde

Moosewood Cookbook by Mollie Katzen

Of Woman Born by Adrienne Rich

Children's and Household Tales by the Brothers Grimm

Medical Muses: Hysteria in Nineteenth-Century Paris by Asti Hustvedt

The Joy of Cooking by Irma S. Rombauer

A Quick Brush of Wings by Mary TallMountain

Susie Sexpert's Lesbian Sex World by Susie Bright

Macho Sluts by Pat Califia

The Second Sex by Simone de Beauvoir

Witchcraze: A New History of the European Witch Hunts by Anne Llewellyn Barstow

Discipline and Punish: The Birth of the Prison by Michel Foucault

Borderlands/La Frontera: The New Mestiza by Gloria E. Anzaldúa

This Bridge Called My Back by Cherríe Moraga and Gloria E. Anzaldúa

The Gloria Anzaldúa Reader edited by AnaLouise Keating

Sun, Moon, and Talia by Giambattista Basile

Gender Trouble by Judith Butler

Feminist Theory: From Margin to Center by bell hooks

Revolutionary Letters by Diane di Prima

This Kind of Bird Flies Backward by Diane di Prima

The Poetics of Space by Gaston Bachelard

Naming Our Destiny by June Jordan

Stone Butch Blues by Leslie Feinberg

Sassafrass, Cypress & Indigo by Ntozake Shange

The Epistemology of the Closet by Eve Kosofsky Sedgwick

The Scarlet Letter by Nathaniel Hawthorne

Introduction to Magick by School of Life Design

Empire of the Senseless by Kathy Acker

If Women Counted: A New Feminist Economics by Marilyn Waring

Tell Me a Riddle by Tillie Olsen

Written on the Body by Jeanette Winterson

Acknowledgments

I started writing *We Were Witches* with no clear idea of where I was going with it beyond a few recurring images. I took inspiration and guidance from Katherine Arnoldi, Nina Packebush, Lidia Yuknavitch, Moe Bowstern, Sailor Holladay, Rhiannon Dexter Flowers, Allison McCarthy, Megan Kruse, China Martens, Megan Moodie, Jenny Forrester, Jessica Lawless, Joe Zirker, and Justin Hocking.

Michelle Gonzales, Karin Spirn, and Tomas Moniz listened to draft after draft and said, "You can trust that structure. You can trust that."

Deena made me strong coffee and perfect poached eggs. She and Max and I all live in a studio apartment. It turns out you can write books without a room of your own.

Zoe Zolbrod published a couple of early excerpts from the project in the *Rumpus* and emboldened me to keep going. Maybe the world of stories could welcome a teen/twentysomething mom with a complicated narrative.

I sent the draft to Michelle Tea, and she said, "*Absolutely!*"

Jennifer Baumgardner acted as though the Feminist Press had been waiting its whole life just for this book. I dig it when people act like that.

The rest of the wonderful team at the Feminist Press—Lauren Hook, Alyea Canada, Drew Stevens, Suki Boynton, Wren Hanks, Jisu Kim, Leah Fry, Lucia Brown, and Hannah Goodwin—each added their particular magic: care with words, care with images.

Love and care, it turns out—love and care and public art—are the antidotes to shame.

My daughter, Maia, has had the odd experience of being a character in my stories and books her whole life. She's an excellent traveling companion, and I so appreciate her kindness and good humor about the whole mama-writer thing.

Here's hoping Max is also amused.

The Feminist Press is a nonprofit educational organization founded to amplify feminist voices. FP publishes classic and new writing from around the world, creates cutting-edge programs, and elevates silenced and marginalized voices in order to support personal transformation and social justice for all people.

See our complete list of books at
feministpress.org